'GOD SAVE THE KING'

by
Terry Cavender

DEDICATION

To my beloved Mags and Sara,
and also to Tom Balch and
Mike Walters for their
advice and assistance

'The midnight agony of things undone'
L.A.G. Strong

COPYRIGHT

CHAPTERS

12. IT'S NOT MY BAG.

13. DOUBLE DEALING.

14. PRESIDENT XI JIANG HO WILL SEE YOU NOW.

15. IS THIS BUCKINGHAM PALACE?

16. MIND THE GAP!

'GOD SAVE THE KING'

CHAPTER ONE

'A MOST SENSITIVE TASK'

THIRD (OPERATIONAL) SECTION, MINISTRY OF STATE SECURITY, PEOPLE'S REPUBLIC OF CHINA

The Ministry of State Security (China) is the principal Civilian, Intelligence, Security and Secret Police Agency of the People's Republic of China. The Agency shares its Headquarters with the Ministry of Public Security, right next to the infamous Tiannamen Square, at 14 Dongchangan Avenue, Dongcheng District, Beijing. An area to be avoided.

A wizened, haggard, but still fearsome Lieutenant General Tang Zhi Peng, the impressively titled Head of the Intelligence Bureau, Third (Operational) Section, Ministry of State Security (MSS) for the People's Republic of China, felt a long forgotten surge of excitement coursing through his ancient, clogged up veins. At long last his master plan to strike a knock-out blow at the British, whom he had despised for more years than he cared to remember, was about to be implemented.

Lieutenant General Tang knew that despite the youthful and loathsome Chinese President, Xi Jiang Ho, not having given his tacit approval for such an operation to be formulated to strike at the very heart of the despised so called 'British Establishment,' the General would undoubtedly be able to bask in the glory of its success, once it had been completed successfully. Tang always worked on the premise - 'Better to ask for forgiveness than seek permission' which was OK when everything went as planned. General Tang Zhi Peng was convinced that when the relatively young President was faced with a fait accompli - once the British Monarch, King George the Seventh, had been assassinated. President Xi would have no other option but to approve, albeit retrospectively.

The vindictive old curmudgeon Lieutenant General Tang nursed a deeply seated hatred for the British and all that they represented, especially the English, particularly after him having served undercover in the London based People's Republic of China Embassy at Portland Place for a number of years. Easily slighted, the General, who had been a lowly Captain back in the day, had consistently taken offence at what he'd regarded as being gratuitous insults and the condescending treatment being larded on Chinese citizenry by the 'chinless wonders' employed at the British Ministry of Defence and their inefficient self-seeking Civil Service.

Like an elephant, Tang never forgot or forgave those who had delivered the stinging 'slaps.' It was in his nature to nurse grudges for years and he'd taken great enjoyment in formulating plans to wreak some sort of terrible revenge on them. Now a very senior and important officer in his own right, Lieutenant General Tang was in a position to achieve his aims.

His very pretty Military Assistant, the petite and perfectly formed Captain Zhou Min Zhia, smiled, bowed her head and said quietly in her sing-song voice, "General, my sincere apologies for disturbing you, but I thought you should know that Lieutenant Colonel Weng Hang Soon has arrived in the outer office." The General took a final suck on the soggy end of his preferred foul smelling Chinese 'Nanjing Twelve Ladies King-size' cigarette then ground the stub of it out in the overflowing ashtray at the centre of his cluttered desk before snapping back at her, "Well then, we'd better not keep him waiting, had we, Captain Zhou! Bring him in here!"

As the Captain turned and sashayed out of his office, deliberately provoking him imagined the drooling General, he admired her perfect figure and decided that she would share dinner and his bed with him that very evening. He had lost his long suffering wife many years ago and since then had been free to enjoy the lascivious fruits of his favoured position in the Chinese hierarchy. Rank definitely had its privileges.

Tang fired up his lap-top and tapped out a quick e-mail instructing Captain Zhou Min Zhia to reserve his usual private suite at the Senior

Officers' Club and also invited her along to join him, knowing that she would hardly be in a position to refuse. "It will be a most memorable night for her; indeed it will be for both of us," he thought, "and if she meets with my expectations, I will then confirm her promotion to Major." The randy old goat smiled to himself, licked his wet, thin, blood-blistered lips and then tapped the 'send' button. Now, though, it was time for him to get down to business with Lieutenant Colonel Weng.

The office door opened and Captain Zhou entered, closely followed by an apprehensive looking Lieutenant Colonel Weng Hang Soon. "General Tang, I have the honour, sir, to present Lieutenant Colonel Weng Hang Soon," trilled Captain Zhou. Lieutenant Colonel Weng halted smartly in front of the General's desk and threw him a snappy parade ground style salute. The General totally ignored him for the statutory two minutes, simply because he could, then said, "Remove your headdress and take a seat, Weng" indicating a chair at the side of his desk.

He then waved a nicotine stained hand dismissively at Captain Zhou, who quickly left the office, closing the door quietly behind her, greatly relieved to be away from close proximity to General Tang. In truth, the lecherous General made her skin crawl and she hated being anywhere near him. He had wandering hands. Tang's red-rimmed eyes, enlarged unnaturally by the lenses on his 'John Lennon' style spectacles, consistently roved up and down her body, mentally undressing her whilst she was standing in front of his desk. Unfortunately, she hadn't had the opportunity to read the General's e-mail yet so didn't know that a rather unpleasant night awaited her. She would have little choice other than to accept the invitation, so would eventually just have to lie back and think of China.

The General, an eighty cigarettes a day man, lit yet another cigarette and said, "I would offer you one, Weng, but I am aware that you do not indulge in such perceived weaknesses." Lieutenant Colonel Weng leapt to his feet, startling the old General, "That is correct, I do not smoke, but I do not criticise those that do, General." "Would you please refrain from popping up and down like a 'Jack in the Box' every time I address you, Weng. It is most disconcerting. Remain seated until I instruct you to do otherwise," said General Tang.

"My sincere apologies, General," said Weng, lowering himself back down onto the chair and sitting there unmoving and ramrod straight.

"Now, Weng, you must be wondering why I have summoned you here into my inner office?" said the General. Before Lieutenant Colonel Weng could open his mouth to reply, the General continued, "As time flies like an arrow, I will get straight to the point. I have a very sensitive task for you to undertake. It is highly classified, is of national importance and will have severe repercussions at the very highest level should anything goes wrong - which it had better not do or we will both suffer the undoubtedly unfortunate consequences!" he said, giving a meaningful nod towards the life-size portrait of the President and Commander in Chief of the People's Republic of China, Xi Jiang Ho, that was mounted on the wall directly opposite him.

"Based upon your recent commendable achievements, you, Weng, I have selected you personally to undertake a particularly ultra-sensitive task because I know that you are an officer well able to get things done, no matter what the challenges or difficulties may present themselves. For instance, you did particularly well with the South Korean business," he laughed until he coughed, spat into a grubby handkerchief, then continued, "particularly as the Americans finished up getting the blame for the nuclear explosion. Even our beloved President was impressed. It was indeed a job well done. Shame about South Korea, although they will recover in about a hundred years. An impressive performance." "Thank you, General. I am deeply honoured that both you and our President should think so." replied a faintly embarrassed Lieutenant Colonel Weng, nearly standing up.

General Tang reached across his desk and opened the slim file that was laid directly in front of him. The file had a bold red cross stencilled across its front and back covers, indicating that it was 'Cosmic Top Secret - Leadership Eyes Only.' After taking a few minutes to theatrically leaf through the contents of the file, Tang said, "In essence, Weng, you have been selected to attend a General Transport Course at the British Army's Defence School of Transportation - 'DST' - a large military establishment that is tucked away in a corner of the poverty stricken North of England. You will be going there as part of an official 'Officer Exchange Programme.' You will know, I'm sure, that we send two of our Army officers over there annually, and similarly they send two of their officers over here, each of us ostensibly to study the others transport methods - but in reality both groups using the opportunity to gather useful information which would not normally be available to us."

He puffed on his cigarette, filling his office with clouds of foul smelling smoke, then continued, "Naturally, you will be under deep cover for the duration of the attachment, as Captain Weng Hang Soon, a rather lowly Transport Officer. You need not fear, it is only a temporary demotion to Captain, I assure you. The British have no idea who you are, as we have made sure that your name has never appeared on any of our Army Lists or official documents. You will be detached to the 'DST' for a period of approximately three months, ostensibly to study the various means of administrative transport currently in use by the British Army, or what is left of it, and study their training methods. There will be another officer nominated to accompany you, name yet to be decided, but that officer will be a female. She will be unaware of your true identity and why you are really there. The British, will also be clueless, as is normal for them. The British, huh, I don't know why they are so full of themselves, we have more soldiers looking after our latrines than the British Army has as an entity. Why, even the Polish Army is three times larger than the pathetic British one!"

Weng sniggered dutifully as the General continued, "They inevitably fail to remember their history - 'Study the past if you would define the future!' They have foolishly cut their military to the bone so that now their Army is smaller now than when Napoleon fought them. The British shoot themselves in the foot every time." Weng nodded and thought to himself, "Yes, General, but remember what happened to Napoleon!"

Droning on, Tang continued, "Do you know Weng, the British Government spends more sending us 'overseas aid' each year than they expend on their own military budget! The arrogance of them sending us 'overseas aid.'" General Tang laughed, his laugh turning into a rattling, phlegm ridden graveside wheeze.

Once he'd regained his breath, the gasping General continued, "Obviously, Weng, studying transport and training methods is not the real reason you are being sent to such a god-forsaken place, you being one of our most highly skilled security operatives. Before I continue, however, I should warn you, Weng, that what I am about to tell you is classified as 'Cosmic Top Secret - Leadership Eyes Only.' In the hopefully unlikely event that a single word of it leaks out, you and your family, and by that I mean <u>all</u> of them, will be taken into custody and will then vanish from the face of the earth. Heads will roll. Naturally, you will be required to sign a document to that effect. Is that clearly understood?!"

Lieutenant Colonel Weng nodded and answered, "Perfectly, General" a thin bead of sweat suddenly appearing on his top lip. "Where the hell is all this pointless threatening leading?" Weng wondered, "And he must know that I'm an orphan, so there is no-one else that can be punished. An empty and pointless threat!"

The General nodded approvingly, "Very well, in which case, let us continue. In a nutshell, whilst you are at 'DST,' you are going to plan and oversee the assassination of the exceedingly corrupt British King George the Seventh, who as you may or may not know has become something of a thorn in our side, particularly regarding the Taiwan question." Weng's jaw dropped as the General continued, "Even before he was crowned he promoted dangerous western values and in continuing to do so, undermines our beloved President by criticising the 'Chinese Dream' and mocking our attempts at cultural revival in a land that is rightfully ours."

The General's reedy voice went an octave higher as he began to rant, "Taiwan rightfully belongs to China." He lit yet another cigarette and continued, "And I am convinced that our beloved President will resolve that particular issue before too long, as he did with Hong Kong."

General Tang, wheezing like an accordion, drew heavily on his cigarette before continuing, "Obviously your first thoughts will be - "Why the Defence School of Transportation at Leconfield and not, say, the capital city of London? Well, 'pin back your ears' as the despised English say and let me explain. Obviously, His Majesty the King is too closely guarded whilst he is in London and it is nigh on impossible to get near to him, but when he leaves there, which he does with great frequency, it then becomes a horse of a different colour. From an impeccable source at our London Embassy, we have been informed that the King is scheduled to visit 'DST' Leconfield, and rather fortuitously, it will be whilst you are in situ there.

Now, come over here and have a look at this file, Weng. You will not be able to take it out of my office and so must commit its entire contents to memory, which will not be too difficult for you as I know that you are fortunate enough to have been gifted with a photographic memory. Oh, and by the way, a bonus. On this occasion his ridiculous Queen will be accompanying him. So, using the modern vernacular, it will be a 'TWOFERS' operation."

Weng looked slightly puzzled. The General smiled and explained, "TWOFERS' - means that we'll get two for the price of one!"

CHAPTER TWO

'WE'RE OFF 'OOP NORTH!'

His cheeks turning puce, buggers grips bristling, the spluttering King George the Seventh hurtled his favourite egg spoon down onto the pristine white table cloth, splattering it with egg yolk from his free range pheasant egg. His meaty clenched fist crashed onto the table as he bellowed, "We point blank refuse to apologise!" From a good twenty feet away at the other end of the breakfast table, Queen Margaret glanced up at him, smiled graciously and called out, "Erm, is that 'You and Me,' - or just the 'Royal We,' Georgie?" "It's the 'Royal We,' Margot," replied the King. "So, what's fired your rockets this early in the day then?" the Queen asked him, "Not the 'Ginger Whinger' again I hope!" The King shook his head and explained, "No, it's not our Bertie - not this time anyway." "Well, what is it then?" the Queen asked, "It must be something out of the ordinary if it's making you chuck your favourite spoon across the breakfast table?"

The King took a long, deep breath to help calm himself, then continued, "I'm sorry, dear, it's the morning newspapers don't you see. If I might explain. Many moons ago, back in the good old days when I was a young Prince of Wales, must be some fifty years ago now, I wrote a letter of support to the then Australian Prime Minister, Gerard Crampton, just after Mummy's Governor-General, Sir Andrew Norton, had peremptorily sacked him without reference to the Queen, which both she and I thought was unconstitutional and most outrageous. Well, the contents of my letter were leaked by some scallywag, which caused a considerable amount of hoo-hah at the time. You see, the Governor General had, in my humble opinion, dropped a right bollock by not seeking the Queen's permission, and he should have been summoned to London to account for his actions. Would you believe that when the gutter press found out about my little note they had the impertinence to accuse me of behaving with impropriety for writing to poor old Mr Crampton - as if I would do that! Quite the opposite, if anything!"

"A spot of hoo-hah, you say!" said the Queen, "Well, if memory serves, it was a tad more than hoo-hah, Georgie - more of an all-singing, all-dancing constitutional crisis?" Queen Margaret laid her freshly ironed copy of 'The Daily

Grafter' down and spooned some more Manuka honey-drizzled porridge into her mouth, "Huh, it's a storm in a bloody tea cup I suppose. Much worse things happen at sea," said the King, shaking his head, "But I was merely doing the right and proper thing, expressing a little sympathy for the poor man, him having been stripped of his rank and slung out on his ear just like that. Mummy was spitting feathers; I can tell you – and I couldn't possible repeat what dear Papa said. You see, all that I did was advise Mr Crampton not to lose heart and stay strong, nothing else, totally non-political. Fat lot of good it did though. I might as well not have bothered. The poor man was slung out on his ear and sank without trace. The last I heard he was breeding kangaroo's on a farm in the outback - and that was that."

The King gave a heartfelt sigh, "Anyway, for some strange reason, the subject has reared its ugly head again and now those bloody Australian Republicans are demanding an apology from me for interfering in their internal affairs, albeit fifty years ago! Well, it's not going to happen, is it. They can go and get stuffed!"

"I suppose you could say that it's 'boomeranged' back on you!" said a smiling Margaret, "and anyway, I've said it before, and I'll say it again, you should concentrate your efforts on things like eradicating Poverty, Disease, 'Badger Culling' or 'Alternative Herbal Medicines.' Much safer than the bottomless swamp that is politics, don't you think!" George tutted loudly, "'Boomeranged back!' Very witty, darling. You know, I cannot, for the life of me, fathom why the bloody gutter press would show an interest in something that happened so many years ago - and now have the impudence to raise the issue all over again!"

He pointed, with a porky, beautifully manicured forefinger, "Look, it's even on the front page of that crappy communist rag you will insist upon reading every day! The Prime Minister, our Prime Minister, could quite easily have had the story spiked. Instead it's plastered all over the front pages – again, as if it's only just happened! That P.M. is bloody useless – even if it were pissing down he couldn't get wet to save his life!" The King sighed, "You know, Margot, these days it seems as if I can't even fart out of tune without somebody commenting on it! They never give me a moment's respite, particularly those red tops."

"You should just do what I do and ignore them all, darling," replied Margaret, "it's just a little ploy that the Editors use to keep their sales figures up. They love a bit of Royal mayhem. Yes, it might well be front page news today, but it'll be wrapping paper for the nation's fish and chips by tomorrow. As you say, a storm in a tea cup, cobber." "Huh," said the King, "whenever my Press Office complains to Fleet Street about these things, all they get back is a melange of dubious justifications from those seedy self-seeking Editors." "You should just dish out a few more knighthoods, darling," said the Queen. The King was twisting his chunky signet ring furiously, "All I am is just a bird in a bloody gilded cage!" "Now drop it down a cog, darling. You know what the Specialist said about your blood pressure - and you're starting to sound just like Basil Fawlty again!" said Margaret.

Not to be placated, the King who looked for all the world as if he'd been sucking a lemon, turned to the breakfast footman, the ever faithful Michael Hosie, who was lurking the statutory three paces behind the King's chair, (listening to the King and Queen talking, but mind elsewhere), and snapped, "And Michael, would you please tell that bandy-legged Bagpiper who is making

23

that infernal caterwauling to stop it and bugger off back to Scotland, and close the window - one can hardly hear one's self think, what with that racket and those Coldstream Guards stamping around shouting obscenities at each other. It's getting beyond a joke - and whilst you're at it, get this bloody breakfast clutter cleared away. There's crumbs everywhere!"

The Queen tapped her teacup with a spoon and called out, "Oh, and Michael, please tell Lukins to put Radio Four on will you." The King sighed, "Oh, not Radio Four again, darling. Don't know why you bother tuning in to that nest of woke, tree hugging, sandal wearing, left wing hoodies. Huh, the BBC's never been the same since Ken Bruce got hoofed. No wonder they lost the license fee!" "Ken wasn't 'hoofed' at all, my darling. He was made an offer he couldn't refuse and moved on to pastures anew!" said Margaret, "I still tune in to him now and again - he's as fabulouso as ever."

"I wish that we could move on to pastures anew," said the King as he reached across to the precious gem studded solid gold fruit bowl, a present to him from the late President of Russia, Vladimir Putin, and selected a ripe plum, examined it closely then sank his teeth into it. Some of the purple juice squirted from the polished fruit, dribbled down his chin and then splashed onto his light blue silk tie, staining it badly. "Buggeration, that tie was a present from Anne. I'll have to have it sponged off before she spots it or I'll never hear the end of it! She's got eyes like an SAS sniper." As he dabbed at the tie with his napkin, he sighed, "The day's going downhill rapidly."

Queen Margaret smiled, "Cheer up, my love, don't forget that we've got our trip to Yorkshire to look forward to later on today." "Yorkshire?" he grumbled. "Now come on, you rather like it up there, don't you. So, where is it we're going to? I was briefed but I can't for the life of me remember?"

Reaching across and opening the slim briefing file that was laid on the table in front of him, George said, "Let me see now, these notes state that we're paying a visit to the Defence School of Transportation, commonly referred to as 'DST,' up at a place called Leconfield in the East Riding of Yorkshire. It's near the county town of Beverley. We're going up there to have a look at the lads and lasses training on some of the new 'Lend Lease' American vehicles apparently. Whilst we're there, you'll be blistering off to, er, let me see, to a charming little hamlet called 'Wilfsholme,' which is just down the road from Leconfield, to declare a new sewage works open."

The Queen smiled, "A new sewage works, eh. Well, as long as they don't expect me to take the first pee!" Ignoring her, the King continued, "My sister normally does the military transport side of things, but she's gone off to Scotland with hubby Gerald to watch the rugby final. Lucky old things. Anyway, as we'd got a spare couple of hours in our diaries, I volunteered our services to stand in for her. Got to keep our hours up. Oh, and whilst we're 'oop' there, I'll be presenting the Commandant of the School, Brigadier something or other, with a CBE for his work ensuring that lots of new trees were planted on the MOD estate. So, it's a jolly well done to him!"

The King smiled, "You know, I do so love presenting baubles and dishing out knighthoods, and the joy of it is that it doesn't cost me a brass farthing."

The Queen dropped her newspaper onto the floor, and sighed, "Wilfsholme. A new sewage works, eh, that'll be riveting," she said, "Do you know,

George, I haven't opened a sewage works for at least a month! I must have a word with our planning office. For some reason, I always seem to get the crap jobs." George laughed, "That's because you're a Number Two!" "Georgie, what a wag you are!" said Queen Margaret. He smiled, "Come and sit up here, darling," patting the chair next to him.

As they sat there chatting, the King suddenly paused as he recognised the sound of a Sikorski helicopter, its two powerful T64-GE-6 Turboshaft engines noisily throbbing, despite being cloaked by noise suppressors, as it hovered over his back garden. The sound filtered through the now closed breakfast room window.

"Huh," said George, "we have triple glazing installed all over the bloody palace, and despite what the experts say, it still doesn't do anything to reduce the racket! Suppose it's the chopper come to fly us up to Yorkshire," said the King, standing up and looking at his wristwatch, "I'd better go and change this tie. Don't forget that we're leaving at 10.30 hours on the dot, darling. We can read those briefing notes on the way up there if you'd prefer. There's only two pages of them anyway - and that includes our speeches"

"Well it won't take me long to say, 'I declare these bogs open!'" said the Queen, smiling and waving regally.

"Now don't do yourself down, darling, you're a first class speaker. You're so good that you can coach a tear out of a glass eye! Now, I must get on. Would you excuse me," said the King. "You are excused, Your Majesty," said the Queen, her eyes twinkling, "but not until I've had a good morning kissy-wissy!" The King sighed, "Another one! Oh, very well."

He dabbed his mouth with a crisp, 'G7' monogrammed white napkin then leant across to the Queen and gave her a quick peck on the lips. "Oh, you still make my toes curl, George," she whispered seductively, smiling as she caught a whiff of the King's heady 'Highbridge Bouquet' aftershave. The King glanced down surreptitiously at the half empty glass of red claret that the Queen had brought with her from the other end of the table, sighed inwardly, and thought, "Claret and porridge. The Monarchy is doomed!" "I'll meet you in the back garden in half an hour or so then, my darling," said the Queen. "OK. TTFN, Margot," replied the King.

"TTFN, Georgie," replied Margaret, winking at him.

The pilot of the maroon coloured six seater Sikorsky S-76C+ twin engine helicopter, Wing Commander Malcolm King, turned to his co-pilot, Squadron Leader Tony Whittingstall, and said, "I'll just pop her down here, Tony, well away from those damned flower beds. My predecessor made the mistake of landing too close to that segment of the garden and in doing so the downdraft uprooted several exotic plants that the King had planted personally, thereby earning himself a job commanding three Senior Aircraftsmen and several sheep at a radar station in the Outer Hebrides, the poor sod!"

The chopper had flown directly to Buckingham Palace from RAF Northolt, where it was parked up and regularly maintained by 32 (The Royal) Squadron who had sole responsibility for the King's Helicopter Flight. Flight clearance for that day's activities had been granted by RAF Central Command Air Control and a 'Purple Passage' route had been declared by them, which made things so much easier for the chopper pilots, as no other aircraft, commercial or military, were allowed to stray into their allocated 'Royal' airspace on pain of having their flying licence revoked.

As the Sikorski settled gently and expertly onto the closely clipped lawn, slightly to the side of a small square of fluorescent orange material pinned securely to the grass, the pilot powered the engines down and then switched everything to standby. Removing his kid gloves and turning to his co-pilot he said, "Right Tony, we'd better carry out a final check of the aircraft, internal and external, and make sure that everything's tickety-boo. You do the inside and I'll have a walk around the outside. We don't want to be dropping any clangers with this particular pair of VIP's. That would definitely be a career stopper!"

The flight from London to Normandy Barracks, situated just outside the pleasant little village of Leconfield in East Yorkshire, was scheduled to take an hour and a half, and in the unlikely event that they arrived in the area slightly earlier than expected, the pilot planned to fly a couple of circuits around the market town of Beverley to ensure that they landed at the Leconfield base precisely on time. He knew from previous experience that the King would appreciate an ariel view of the magnificent Beverley Minster, so that would get him some 'Brownie points.'

The pilot jumped down from the helicopter, walked slowly around its exterior, examining it closely, then strode across the closely cropped lawn to meet the King's Personal Security Officer, Chief Inspector Peter McGrath who was stood watching him. "Hello again, Peter," said the Wing Commander, smiling, "Nice to see you." The steely eyed Chief Inspector smiled back at him as they shook hands, "Thanks, and nice to see you too, Malcolm."

"Well," said the Wing Commander, "today's visit 'Oop North' should be straightforward enough, eh. The weather's nice and clear. So, what's himself doing up in East Yorkshire then?" Peter replied, "His Majesty is remaining in barracks to play with some of the Army's new toys, whilst Her Majesty the Queen will be nipping off base briefly to open a sewage facility, somewhere out in the sticks, after which they'll both be meeting up and having tea and stickies at the Officers' Mess. His Majesty will then be presenting the base's Commandant with a gong, a CBE I think, before we fly back down here to Buck House. That's it in a nutshell really."

Chief Inspector McGrath continued, "Yes, it'll be a bit of a busy day for all of us. After the Leconfield visit, their Majesties are scheduled to return directly here and then this evening they're attending a Royal Command Performance at the London Palladium, so we can't afford any delays or glitches. You know how twitchy His Majesty gets about timings. He hates inconveniencing people. As usual, their schedule's been timed to the second and he's forever peeping surreptitiously at his wristwatch."

The Chief Inspector indicated the man stood at his side, "By the way, Malcolm, this chap here is Inspector Tom Balch. Tom will be responsible for Her Majesty once she leaves the Leconfield base today. They'll be accompanied by the usual armed local Police Response Team, naturally. I'll be sticking with the King throughout." Tom Balch smiled and shook hands with the pilot, "Pleased to meet you, Wing Commander," he said. "Pleasure's all mine, old boy," said the pilot,

"Right, well if you chaps want to jump on board the chopper and have a bit of a sniff around, please feel free to do so. I'll go and book in with the King's Equerry. The co-pilot's on board the chopper if you have any queries. We had the standard police sniffer dog search before we left Northolt and were given the all-clear. The aircraft hasn't been left unattended since then." "Thanks, old chap," said Chief Inspector McGrath, "come on then Tom, follow me and I'll show you how the other half travels."

The Sikorski helicopter had been designed to carry six passengers in comfort and with the addition of luxury fixtures and fittings was very impressive. Scheduled to be on board for that day's flight would be the King, the Queen, the King's Equerry, Major Adrian Longman QGM, and the Queen's Companion, a very jolly Lady Sara Langthorne - the Marchioness of Robroyston, along with the two Close Personal Security Officers, Peter McGrath and Tom Balch, both of whom were armed - and decidedly dangerous. The two Security Officers would stick to the Royals like glue until they returned to Buckingham Palace at the end of the day's activities..

The Commandant of the Defence School of Transportation (DST) at Leconfield, Brigadier Peter Chambers-Renton, was stood, hands on hips, posing and gazing out of the large Operations Room window at 'E Flight' 202 SAR

(Search and Rescue) Squadron, which was situated in a far corner of DST at Normandy Barracks. In a previous existence, Normandy Barracks had been a large RAF base, designated as RAF Leconfield, until that was, the Army took it over and changed the name of the place to Normandy Barracks. The RAF element still operated from their little corner of the base and clung tenaciously to the nomenclature 'RAF Leconfield' - refusing point blank to change it whenever the Army whinged.

The Brigadier peered at the Operations Room clock, then turned to his Chief of Staff, the unflappable Lieutenant Colonel Sean Lacy, and said, "OK Sean, we've just been informed by the 'Brylcreem Boys' Central Ops Room at Waddington that their Majesties are due to land here in precisely ten minutes. You'd better go and warn the Lord Lieutenant and the Chief Constable off." The Chief of Staff nodded, "Right away, Brigadier," and marched smartly off to the nearby Crew Rest Room where the Official Reception Party, the Lord Lieutenant of the East Riding of Yorkshire, Lady Elizabeth Fenton-Garner CBE, and the Chief Constable of Humberside Police, doughty Scotsman Sir Michael Fraser QPM, were having tea and shortcake biscuits, whilst chatting animatedly with members of the RAF's SAR Standby Duty Crew.

Meanwhile, back in the Leconfield RAF Ops Room, the Commandant DST turned to the OC 'E' Flt, (*Officer Commanding 'E Flight'*), Squadron Leader Harry Connolly, and said, "Right, Hazza, it's over to you and your lads for the landing 'technicals.' I'll go and wait over by the landing pad with the others."

The Lord Lieutenant had just finished telling a salty joke by saying, "And the Lord Mayor said to the Secretary of State, 'Well if you're the smartest person in the room - then you're in the wrong room!'" and the listeners creased up with laughter.

"Forgive my interruption, Ma'am, Sir Michael," said the Chief of Staff, "but we've just been informed by Central RAF Air Ops that their Majesty's helicopter will be landing here in precisely ten minutes. Apparently the pilot will be flying a couple of circuits around Beverley Minster before they touch down here, so as the Minster's just down the road, in theory we should be able to hear the chopper long before we see it."

"Ah, that's excellent news, so there's just time for me to go and open the bomb doors then," bellowed the Lord Lieutenant, (who was as deaf as a post), as she strode off, Miss Marple's like, towards to the ablutions. She paused mid-stride, turned and called out to no one in particular, "Fear not, chaps, I promise not to despoil the thunderbox that's been reserved solely for the use of the Royals!" then laughed loudly as she walked out of the room, slamming the door behind her.

"I should jolly well hope that she doesn't 'despoil' anything," said the Chief of Staff, "we've only just had the King's personal lavatory seat fitted to the cludgie. It was driven up here yesterday, by special courier, all the way from Buck House!" "Och, that makes it a proper throne room then, laddie!" murmured Michael Fraser, the Chief Constable. They all laughed, dutifully.

The Sikorski helicopter landed at RAF Leconfield precisely on time and once all of the formalities had been completed, and the Media crews had been dealt with, the King and Queen were whisked away in separate vehicles to carry out their allocated tasks. The co-pilot of the Sikorski, Squadron Leader Tony Whittingstall, stayed on board the aircraft as per SOP 22 (*Standard Operating Procedure Number 22*), which in essence was never to leave a Royal aircraft unattended.

A group of armed and very professional looking soldiers from DST were stationed at various points around the exterior of the helicopter, cordoning it off, with instructions to ensure that under no circumstances was it to be approached by anyone not authorised to do so. Because it was a Royal visit, their weapons were loaded with live ammunition and they had been given authority to open fire if ordered to do so, or if the circumstances dictated it.

Whilst the Royals were out and about completing their various segments of the visit programme, the Sikorsky's fuel tanks were topped up, ready for the flight back to London. Its exterior was also washed down and then buffed up by an enthusiastic RAF team who had been bussed in from RAF Waddington, as per 'SOP 37 for Royal Aircraft.' Aircraft carrying the Royal family always had to look their absolute best, as they were representing Great Britain, and the specialised team knew exactly what was required.

Major Peter O'Brien, OC MT Div (*Officer Commanding Motor Transport Division*), at DST, unlocked his desk drawer, opened it and pulled out a small cigarette packet sized metal container. Although he didn't know it, the specially designed container contained sufficient high powered explosives to blow a huge hole in both him and his office. He was under the mistaken impression that it was just an electronic bugging device. O'Brien slid the container into his trouser pocket and then reached for his beret. Opening his office door, he bellowed, "Sarn't Major, is my staff car ready?" "Yizzah!" came the reply, "It's out the front of the building waiting for you!" "OK, well I'm off over to E Flight to check up on the armed guards." "Want me to accompany you, sah?" asked the Sergeant Major, "No, I don't, thank you. I'm quite capable of checking them myself. You hold the fort back here!" replied the Major as he stomped off towards his staff car. "Wonder what's up with that sour-faced fart," mumbled the Sergeant Major.

Major O'Brien was an extremely embittered man. At one time, not all that long ago, he had been extremely well thought of and was deemed by his superiors to be heading for greater things, career wise. That was until an unfortunate incident early one morning whilst he was travelling along the autobahn in West Germany, when was leading a convoy of Tank Transporters off on manoeuvres and heading towards a training area near Bielefeld.

O'Brien had carelessly flicked a still glowing cigarette butt out of his Land Rover window, which when the wind had caught it, was blown it back through the window and into the rear of his vehicle. The vehicle, unusually, was carrying the large amount of ammunition and flares allocated for the military exercise.

For some inexplicable reason, the box of flares had been left with its lid slightly ajar and the sparks from the cigarette butt had fallen into the box and ignited a flare, which then promptly set fire to the other flares, the conflagration quickly spreading to the several boxes of ammunition and then the back of the Land Rover, until reaching the fuel tank. The resultant conflagration caused chaos on the autobahn and it was completely blocked for several hours, much to the fury of the German Autobahn Polizei, (and Major O'Brien's fiery Commanding Officer when he heard about it via the incident being headlined on the German TV's premier news show – 'Der Sachsenspiegel.'

The Major was extremely fortunate not to have been court martialled, nevertheless he did not get off lightly. A few days later he had been relieved of his command personally by the GOC (General Officer Commanding) of his Division and immediately posted back to the United Kingdom to the Defence School of Transportation (DST) at Normandy Barracks, Leconfield in East Yorkshire.

It had been agreed with the DST Commandant that Major O'Brien would be permitted to serve a one year shortened tour and then would be required to resign his commission and retire quietly with a greatly reduced pension and a mere fraction of his expected gratuity, never to be seen or heard from again.

O'Brien's disgruntled and highly embarrassed wife, Jenny, the shame of the autobahn incident, everyone sniggering and pointing at her as if she had been responsible, was the straw that finally broke the marital camel's back, so she had packed her bags and left him, taking their young daughter with her. The wife and child were now living in much reduced circumstances in a run-down surplus married quarter on the outskirts of Bulford and were classed as being 'Illegal

Occupants.' They would only be allowed to stay there for a couple of months or so before being evicted, then their accommodation would become a problem.

The shock and disgrace of it all had been almost too much for Major O'Brien to bear and it had badly affected his state of mind, (although no one recognised that at the time because he put up a brave front). He was at the very edge of suffering a mental breakdown and should at the very least have been receiving counselling. Instead, he was just permitted to 'soldier on.' Shockingly, counselling was deemed by his contemporaries to be for 'lower deck' wimps and certainly not for commissioned officers, who were expected to be made of much sterner stuff.

The Chinese People's Army had sought and been given approval for two of their commissioned officers to be detached to and trained at 'DST' Leconfield for several months, as part of a standard Foreign Office Reciprocal Agreement, one whereby China and the UK exchanged military students, (*a.k.a. spies*), under the guise of them undergoing familiarisation training on each other's military transport equipment and studying their day to day administrative routines. One of those nominated Chinese officers was Lieutenant Colonel Weng Hang Soon, (although for the purposes of the exchange visit he was only rated as a lowly Transport Captain, so as not to draw any undue attention to himself). The other Chinese officer was an actual Transport Officer who knew nothing of Weng Hang Soon's true mission.

Not long after his arrival at Leconfield, the now 'Captain' Weng Hang Soon had been seated next to Major O'Brien at a Regimental Dinner Night where O'Brien had got monumentally pissed, had lowered his guard and started speaking about sensitive matters that he certainly shouldn't have done , especially in front of an unfriendly foreign national. The Chinese Captain listening to him burbling on, quickly assessed that O'Brien was far beyond disgruntled and was therefore an ideal candidate with whom to encourage some form of disaffection and was 'ripe for the plucking.'

The MSS Branch (*Ministry of State Security*), of the Chinese PLA (*People's Liberation Army*), had detached Lieutenant Colonel Weng Hang Soon from their Joint Staff Department's Intelligence Bureau, in order to free him up for a highly secretive deep-cover operation at DST

Leconfield. Weng was thrilled at having been given the heaven-sent opportunity and was determined to make a success of it. He would begin by collating as much useful low-grade information from his British hosts as he could manage, without them latching on to what he was really up to. Before leaving China, he had been informed by General Tang Zhi Peng, that if the British King's assassination operation was successful, at the very least it would mean a swift step up the promotion ladder for Weng, probably to the heady heights of Senior Colonel or beyond - a huge jump for someone so relatively junior.

So, as he had been trained and briefed to do, Weng had gone all out to establish a close relationship with Major O'Brien, to whose department he was attached for driver training, and spent a great deal of time with him socially. Rather conveniently, their rooms were situated on the same floor of the Officers' Mess accommodation and more often than not they shared a beer together, sometimes a crisp Chinese 'Tsing Tsao' when they could get hold of it, in the downstairs 'Scruffs Bar' of the Officers' Mess whilst watching sport in the TV lounge.

Whenever Major O'Brien was chatting to him, Captain Weng laughed in all of the right places and enthusiastically agreed with everything he said. Unfortunately for Major O'Brien, he had forgotten the tried and tested adage - 'Never trust a man who laughs too easily.'

Weng worked ultra hard at cultivating a firm friendship with O'Brien. They had even travelled down to London together one weekend, ostensibly for a spot of sight-seeing, as Weng claimed to have never been there, (although he had). After going to see a variety show at the London Palladium, the cunning Weng had taken O'Brien to a Chinese funded night club in a seedier part of Soho that was well off the main tourist route, where O'Brien's drinks had been spiked with Rohypnol.

Once he'd slid into helpless unconsciousness, O'Brien was carried upstairs to a bedroom, undressed and then photographed from all angles, naked in bed in a series of very compromising situations with two well developed Chinese male prostitutes. He was then dressed and taken back to his hotel room, where the following morning, suffering from a ferocious hangover, he made it clear that he failed to remember anything that had happened to him after the first few drinks. Needless to say, Weng and his masters back at the Intelligence Bureau were delighted at the way things were steadily progressing.

One evening, O'Brien and Weng were sat in the Major's room at Leconfield, chewing the cud. "My dear friend," said Weng, "I feel for you, because you know as well as I do that at the end of this year your people are going to drop you like a hot tomato!" Peter O'Brien gave a weak smile, "I think that you mean a hot potato, Hang Soon." Weng nodded, "Forgive my poor vocabulary, Peter, I'm still on a steep learning curve language wise," he said, "but you know to what I'm referring. Surely they can do something for you?" "Weng, you're farting in a thunderstorm," replied a frustrated and bitter Major O'Brien, "I know as well as you do that I'm being nudged towards the exit door. Those bastards can't get rid of me soon enough - and after all that I've been through and the loyalty I've shown them. Northern Ireland, the Falklands, Afghanistan, Aldershot, and not only that, but my marriage is also in tatters and my beautiful little daughter is not allowed to speak to me. All that because of one silly little mistake I made whilst travelling on the German autobahn, something that could have happened to anyone!"

"Have you decided what you are going to do with yourself once you leave the Army? Have you made any other plans yet?" queried Weng. Major O'Brien shook his head, "No, not really. I'll probably be a shelf-filler at Aldi or something. To be honest, I've been putting off thinking about it. One thing I do know, though, is that I'm going to find it incredibly difficult having to exist on the pathetic pension that I'll qualify for, huh, and my wife Jenny is entitled to half of it! As for the lump sum, the so-called 'gratuity' that I'll receive, it'll be risible. I've read the financial projections and there won't even be enough left for me to be able to put a caravan roof over my head once my wife gets her share of that as well, never mind buying bricks and mortar. I won't even be able to raise enough for a deposit on a garden hut! Let's face it Hang Soon, my friend, I'm well and truly up shit creek without a paddle!"

A crafty look slid across Weng's features, "let me be perfectly honest with you, Peter, I am aware of your problems, and if you'll forgive me, I have been giving this matter a great deal of thought. You see, I am in a position where I might be able to help you, my friend. We are friends, aren't we?" said Weng "Of course we are!" replied O'Brien, "You said that you can help me? Help me in what way?" he asked Weng. "Let me explain," said Weng, glancing around and checking that the room door was closed so that no-one else could overhear their conversation.

Weng continued, "Please listen carefully to what I have to say and think about it before you reply. I am able to offer you a substantial amount of money, but you will be expected to do a little something for me in return, of course" The outraged Major O'Brien jumped to his feet, "Now hang on, mate, before you say anything else, Hang Soon, please don't ask me to do anything illegal or disloyal, because I won't do anything like that! I may well have acted like a complete idiot in the past, but one thing that I am not is a traitor. I love my King and country with a passion!"

"Who mentioned anything about you being a traitor?" said a smiling Hang Soon, immediately trying to placate him, "Sit down and relax, my friend. It's just that, as I said, I am in the fortunate position of being able to offer you some financial assistance. It's no big deal. All I'd have to do in order to justify the outlay would be to tell my paymasters that the money was for additional and unexpected expenses. They expect that sort of thing. I would tell them that I was worming my way into your confidence, and that it was costing me extra money."

"You must have a very generous and gormless Paymaster if he falls for that one!" said O'Brien. "May I respectfully remind you, Peter, my friend, that China has very deep pockets," replied Weng, "So please think about it. I'm only trying to help you."

"OK, so exactly what would I be expected to do, in order to get my sticky paws on some of this 'financial assistance' that you're offering - flog you a couple of state secrets? Even if I could, I wouldn't - and in case you hadn't noticed, Hang Soon, we're both sat here at a bog-standard military driving school in deepest, darkest Yorkshire. It's not exactly MI5 territory up here, is it, and we're not knee deep in state secrets!"

"Listen, my friend," said Hang Soon, "you are over egging the pudding a little. It's nothing like that. What I'm asking you to do is something very simple."   "Oh really, so you've already got something in mind, have you?" Weng nodded, "Yes, I have." "What is it then?" asked O'Brien. "All I would like you to do is place this," he pulled a small, slim metal case out of his pocket and handed it to O'Brien, "somewhere inside the King's helicopter when he visits Leconfield next week." The Major gasped, "How the hell did you find out about the Royal visit? It's 'Need to Know' - and you certainly don't need to know!"

"The details of the King's visit may well be highly classified and sensitive information, but you told me all about it when we were at the last Regimental Dinner." "Oh, did I! Was I pissed?" asked the crestfallen Major. Weng nodded, "Yes, I'm afraid that you had consumed more than your fair share of the grape."

"Oh, bugger it!" said O'Brien, then sighed, "Well, it looks like the damage is done. So, what is that ineffectual looking piece of equipment then?" asked the Major, pointing at the small metal case. "This, it's just a small radio transponder that picks up speech clearly and then speed-transmits it over a very impressive distance. It's the latest bit of miniaturised bugging equipment invented by our Scientists. Very state of the art - even the Americans don't know of its existence. Just as an interesting aside, Peter, the chip it contains is exactly the same one as that which is hidden away inside all of your mobile 'phones here in the UK. You must know that everything you and your citizens say is being recorded, 24 hours a day." "You cheeky bastards!" said Major O'Brien, "I thought that that was just a rumour!"

A smiling Weng continued, "You see, my superiors would be most interested in hearing just what your King thinks about the many and varied vehicles that you are training on here at Leconfield, particularly those that you have on temporary loan from the Americans. For obvious reasons, we are unable to get a close look at them ourselves - particularly as here at DST we have a British Instructor accompanying us at all times. So, if this small piece of bugging equipment, which is completely harmless and untraceable to you by the way, can be hidden somewhere in the Royal helicopter cabin, it will easily pick up everything that's being said by the King on his journey back home and will then be transmitted to our London Embassy. When all is said and done, it's only commercial information, but it would be of immense value to our industrial leaders. So, nothing serious really. It's a relatively simple task, easily and could be quickly done and it could not be traced back to you. Look at it logically, Peter, where can the harm be in my people getting some information on a few Yankee vehicles, eh?"

"Well, you say that, Hang Soon, but it wouldn't be as easy as you seem to think. I can't just go mincing up to the King's chopper, jump on board, slide the device under his seat, then bugger off as if nothing's happened," said Major O'Brien, "If it wasn't so ridiculous I'd split a kipper laughing. You can't even begin to imagine the security that's involved in a Royal visit." "I disagree," said Weng, "You could do it quite easily, my friend. You have already told me that your soldiers will be responsible for guarding the Royal aircraft whilst it is parked up on the landing pad over at RAF Leconfield. As their Officer Commanding, you'll be expected to pay the site a visit, surely? So what's to stop you getting on board the helicopter and hiding the device out of sight somewhere whilst the King and Queen are out and about meeting the 'unfortunates' as they so demeaningly refer to them? It'll only take you a moment or two, using a bit of sleight of hand. No one will notice, and I can promise you a great deal of untraceable cash for carrying out such a simple task. Many hundreds of pounds in used notes that I guarantee will be untraceable. The money would boost your meagre 'gratuity' and help you immeasurably with your retirement plans. It will certainly help you to get a roof over your head if nothing else. This could be the start of a very productive relationship."

"Tell you what, I think that you'd better leave my room, Hang Soon, and we'll both pretend that this ridiculous conversation never happened. You know as well as I do that I'm obliged to report these sort of approaches to our Intelligence and Security boys," said Major O'Brien, "I have no choice." Weng sighed and said, "Very well, if that is your decision, I will respect your wishes. Before I leave, however, perhaps you'd care to cast an eye over these." Weng passed a large brown envelope over to the Major. "What's this?" asked a puzzled O'Brien. "Why not open the envelope and take a look," said Weng Hang Soon. "It had better not be cash! I just told you that I'm not open to accepting a bribe!" said O'Brien. "Oh, it is not a bribe, I can assure you of that," said Weng.

Major O'Brien opened the envelope and slid out several glossy coloured A-5 sized photographs.

After looking at them for a moment, he gasped and sat down, slack jawed, his face as white as a sheet. "Where did you get these from? I don't remember any of this! They're just clever mock-ups aren't they?" Weng shook his head and smiled, "No, they are not mock-ups, my friend. You may recall our recent 'sightseeing' trip to London, when we went nightclubbing in Soho and you got horribly pissed?" O'Brien nodded. "Well," said Weng, "that is when they were taken."

The penny dropped. "Oh no, a honey trap!" gasped O'Brien, "One of the oldest tricks in the book - and I fell for it." "Well, to be fair," said Weng, "you were slipped a hefty dose of Ketamine by the busty bar girl, which helped us considerably, especially when it came to the bedroom posing segment. You were well out of it. Let me put your mind at rest, though, nothing 'physical' happened that night between you and those other two guys - although you wouldn't think so looking at the photos, would you. I rather approve of that photo there, the one of you wearing fishnet tights, although your legs need shaving," he said, pointing, "Quite inventive our chaps, eh! They're specially trained you know. Some of your senior politicians and diplomats keep them very busy." "I ought to smack you in the mouth!" said a furious O'Brien. "Calm down! That will not help," said Weng.

"What are you going to do with the photos" gasped the apprehensive Major. "Well, it's up to you really," replied Weng, "Several sets have been prepared. One set for your wife's Solicitor, one set for your parents, one set for the Commandant here at DST, and one set for your MI5 people in London - and I nearly forgot, we'll probably send copies to the Media, which I'm sure they'll keep to one side for a quiet news day. Oh, and last, but not least, we might just have an enlarged set pinned on the Officers' Mess notice board, the one just outside the main dining room. Everyone who is anyone will get to see them then."

A traumatised Major O'Brien picked up a cigarette packet with trembling hands and fished a cigarette out of it. As he lit it, he mumbled, "And like a fool, I thought that you were my friend, Weng. You've really screwed me over here! I can't believe that I fell for it. You do realise that if those photos are made public I'll become a laughing stock, I'll be disgraced and more than likely kicked out of the Army more or less immediately, probably via the Court Martial Centre at Aldershot. It would also mean that I'd get absolutely no financial compensation, indeed, I'd lose all of my pension and gratuity and more than likely finish up serving time in nick. No one's going to believe that I knew nothing about those photos being taken. I'm in between a rock and a hard place."

"An unfortunate choice of words, Peter. Listen, my friend, stay calm and think about it," said Weng, "There's no need for any of that to happen, is there! Just do the one insignificant little task that I have asked of you and I promise that those photos will never see the light of day again - and you will still receive a generous amount of untraceable money. I give you my word on that!" "Oh, you'll give me your word will you - is that as an officer and gentleman of the Chinese People's Liberation Army! I think not!" said O'Brien, fiercely stubbing the half smoked cigarette out in his ashtray, sending glowing sparks showering over the table top.

"Listen, we all have our duty to do, Pcter, and I am only doing mine. Despite all of this sordid business, I regard you as being a personal friend of mine, you know," said Weng. Shaking his head, O'Brien said, "I should have known better than to trust you, you treacherous little shite-hawk! I'll bet that you're not a Transport Officer either, are you!" Weng smiled and shook his head, "Afraid not." "Oh, what a complete tit I've been," said Major O'Brien, "Well, as if things weren't bad enough already, now I'll be totally wiped out."

There was a few minutes deathly silence, then O'Brien sighed and said to Weng, "Well, Weng, It seems as if I have very little choice, doesn't it. You've cornered me like a rat in a trap. So tell me again about that shitty little piece of equipment and what it can do then."

Weng Hang Soon had to smother the urge to smile. He knew that he now had Major O'Brien well and truly by the short and curlies and that his assassination plan stood a very good chance of succeeding. As he explained about the small metal case once again, he smiled inwardly; he loved it when a good plan started to come together and this was just the tip of the spear.

CHAPTER THREE

'THE ROYAL ARRIVAL'

Major O'Brien's sparklingly shiny Land Rover Discovery staff car drew up at the side of the helicopter landing pad at 'E' Flight, 202 (Search and Rescue) Squadron and after instructing his driver to go and wait for him over in the Admin Area, he then went to check up on his guard detachment. As he was striding around the landing pad area, the door of the helicopter suddenly slid open and an immaculately uniformed Squadron Leader Tony Whittingstall bounded down the red carpeted steps. He called out, "Hello there Major, can I help you?" Peter O'Brien smiled, saluted and held out his hand. "Oh, hi! I'm Peter O'Brien, the OC MT Div here at the School. Those are my chaps guarding your aircraft. I'm just checking up on them to make sure that they're doing the job properly. You can't be too careful, eh!"

The Squadron Leader smiled and shook the Major's hand, "I'm Tony Whittingstall, the co-pilot of this splendiferous machine. Let me assure you that your lads and lasses have been doing a spiffing job. No-one who shouldn't be here has got anywhere near the chopper since their Majesties departed,. Just the RAF refuellers and the spit and polish brigade, that is. Oh, and I mustn't forget the local Police Dog Sniffer Section, they've had a jolly thorough root around too."

The Major smiled and nodded towards the Royal helicopter, "That's a fine looking aircraft you have there, Ian," he said, "It's the first time I've seen a Sikorski so close up." The Squadron Leader smiled, "Yes, we're quite proud of her, she's a bit of a cracker. She's a twin- engine, six seater, Sikorsky S.76C - goes like the clappers too." "Very impressive," said the Major, "I, er, don't suppose I could take a quick peek through the door, could I?"

The Squadron Leader smiled, "Well, we're not supposed to do that sort of thing, but I think that in your case we can do a bit better than that. I can't see any harm in letting you have a quick butchers inside the chopper - brother officer and all that sort of thing. Come on then, Peter, follow me!" "Wow, this is going to be far easier than I could have imagined," thought a delighted Major

O'Brien, feeling for the small metal box in his pocket.

Once inside the helicopter he had a good look around and made all the appropriate appreciative noises. "That's the King's favourite seat over there," said the Squadron Leader, pointing, "He always favours the port side, says he gets a better view out of the window." "Don't suppose I'm allowed to sit in it?" asked O'Brien. "Feel free," replied the Squadron Leader, laughing, "then you can come and have a look around the cockpit if you like."

As the Squadron Leader left the main cabin and entered the cockpit, Major O'Brien eased himself into the King's seat, glanced up at the cockpit to make sure that he wasn't being watched, then slid the small metal case out of his pocket and tucked it down the side of the seat and underneath the beautifully finished leather cushion, well out of sight.

"Whose are these manky old slippers then?" called out the Major. "Oh, those, they're Her Majesty's. She likes to slip them on after completing her walkabouts. She gets them from Harrods," replied the Squadron Leader. "Come up and have a look at the flight deck," he called out. O'Brien eased himself up out of the seat, checked that the metal case couldn't be seen and then went up to the cockpit.

"You might be interested in that bit of Heath Robinson kit over there," said the Squadron Leader, pointing at a complex piece of electrical equipment bolted on to the side of the main instrument panel, "It was only installed quite recently. State of the art actually - even our American brethren across the pond haven't got one!" "Looks very complicated, what does it do?" asked O'Brien.

"Before I explain, I should tell you that it's highly classified at the moment, so please don't mention it to anyone else. It's called '**E.M.B.E.(R)**.' Electronic Military Blocking Equipment - (Radio's) and it does exactly what it says on the tin. It monitors, filters and blocks all illegal incoming radio traffic, and it masks everything that we transmit, obviously in order to stop our outgoing messages, including cell 'phones, being scanned by unauthorised personnel, that sort of thing. Unfortunately, most of the key components come from China, so we have to be careful that there's nothing untoward hidden away inside it."

"Rather defeats the object of the exercise," thought O'Brien. "Can't we produced that sort of thing ourselves?" asked O'Brien. The Squadron Leader shook his head, "No, not really. We don't have the technical expertise, yet. Unfortunately, we're still in the land of valves! Come and sit in the pilot's seat," said the Squadron Leader.

As he eased himself into the pilot's seat, O'Brien smiled and thought, "Looks like I'm out of jail free. Money for old rope!" He'd planted the monitoring equipment, which he presumed now wouldn't work because of **E.M.B.E.(R)** - and the kicker was that both items of equipment had Chinese roots. He had to fight not to laugh out loud. "Thanks for the guided tour, Tony," said O'Brien, "and be assured that my lips are sealed regarding all of the classified aspects of what I've been shown today." He looked at his wristwatch, "I'd better clear off before the Royals get back and ask me what I'm doing up here!" Tony smiled, "Thanks. It's been an absolute pleasure meeting you, old chap." "The next time you're passing this way, do let me know and I'll take you to lunch at the Mess, eh!" said Major O'Brien, "My treat!" Tony winked and they shook hands, "That's a date, mate!"

A happy and relieved Major O'Brien exited the helicopter and strode jauntily across to his waiting staff car, whistling his Corps March. Seeing him approaching, his driver jumped out of the vehicle, saluted and opened the back door of the staff car, "No, it's OK, I'll sit in the front with you, Thurling," he said. "Bloody hell, he's bucked up a bit," thought his driver, "His mood changes like the pigging weather."

When he got back to his office, O'Brien picked up his cell 'phone and rang Weng Hang Soon. "Hi, it's me. You'll be pleased to know that the dirty deed's been done and everything went without a hitch," he said. "Excellent news, and well done, my friend. Now, might I suggest that you get rid of the cell 'phone that you're using. It's a burner." "A burner. What does that mean?" asked O'Brien. "That it's only supposed to be used once and then disposed of. I did mention it to you before." "OK, well I can't be expected to remember everything. I'm new at this covert activities lark. I'll see to it asap," said O'Brien.

"Peter, let's go into Beverley tonight, have some dinner and a quiet chat about today's 'activities,'" suggested Weng. "That's fine with me, but you'll have to cough up for it. I'm afraid I'm boracic," said the Major. "Boracic?" asked Weng. "Yes, Boracic Lint - skint!" "Oh, you needn't worry about that anymore, your financial troubles are now over," said Weng, "Tell you what, I'll meet you at the front entrance of the Mess at seven, if that's OK. We can use my car," said Weng, "then you can have a drink without worrying. Oh, and I'll hand the money over to you."

"Where are we going in Beverley?" asked O'Brien. "To a Chinese restaurant, of course!" replied Weng. "Well, we might be better off going further afield to Cottingham or Hull, it'll be a bit more private there," said O'Brien. "OK," said Weng, "the choice is yours."

CHAPTER FOUR

'BRACE FOR COLLISION!'

The King had decided that he wanted to sit in the co-pilot's seat for the return flight to London, something he did occasionally in order to maintain the hours in his flying log book. As a consequence, Squadron Leader Whittingstall was required to occupy the King's seat in the main body of the helicopter, directly opposite the Queen. "Bloody hell," thought Whittingstall, "this is going to be hard work. What the hell am I going to talk to Her Majesty about for the next hour and a half."

He watched as the Queen eased her Louboutin shoes off and then slipped her throbbing feet into her favourite slippers. "These sodding bunions are a curse," she said. She then opened her handbag, rooted around and pulled out an electronic cigarette. "I'll just have a crafty vape before H.M. arrives," she said, winking at the Squadron Leader, then placing her exclusive 'Anya Hindmarch' cavernous handbag at the side of her seat. "Between you and I, Squadron Leader, I always use cinnamon flavour when I'm vaping. H.M. thinks that it's air freshener!" she laughed and said, "He'll latch on one day though."

As the Sikorski lifted off the Helipad, the King waved to all of the VIP's stood outside the RAF building. "Bloody good fun   today, Wing Commander, what!" he said to the Pilot, "The Lord Lieutenant of the East Riding of Yorkshire's a bit of a character. She's as deaf as a post you know. Kept breaking wind and didn't realise that we could all hear her every emission!" The King laughed, "Now, Wingco, you were going to brief me about something called **E.M.B.E.(R).** I believe?" "Oh, yes sir," said Bellamy, "that's it bolted onto the panel over there, just behind your joystick."   "Incidentally, Wingco, it's very thoughtful of you to fly us back to London via one of those old Forts that still sits quite happily in the Humber Estuary. It's astounding that they're still in one piece, particularly when you consider that even bus stops don't survive these days," said the King. "Right, let's crack on then," said the King. The helicopter circled, then flew away, the VIP's waving merrily, all of them relieved that the Royal visit had been so successful. They were all returning to the Officers' Mess as the

Commandant's guests to continue the celebration for him having received his medal from the King.

"Well, Your Majesty, I hope you don't mind, but I did a bit of research about the particular Fort that we're going to go and have a look at today. It's called the Haile Sand Fort. Thought that you might be interested in some background?" said the Wing Commander. "Oh how spiffing, that's very kind of you. Do tell," replied the King enthusiastically. "Well, sir, the Haile Sand Fort, that's the name of the one that we're going to fly around, was erected in the Humber Estuary during World War One, back in May 1915 actually. It was built there in order to help protect the Humber Estuary from attack by the Germans. It consists of 40,000 tons of concrete and steel and cost the equivalent of £1.5 million pounds at the time. It took four years to build and was completed in 1919. After all of that, apparently it's armaments were never fired in anger." The King smiled, "We must have scared the Boche off!" he said.

The Wing Commander continued, "The Fort stayed operational throughout World War Two and the Army, who had been responsible for manning it, finally left there in 1956, although a small military presence was retained there until the early 1960's. Apparently the Forts are worth about £90 grand now and are up for sale. No takers as yet though." "Bit of a shame that," said the King, "we really should maintain them for posterity. I'll drop the PM a note when I get back home." "It'll probably finish up as a pirate radio station," said the Wing Commander."

'The Haile Sand Fort'

"Well, that was most informative, Wingco, and thank you for taking the time to find it all out," said the King. "That's the miracle of 'Google,' replied the Wing commander. The King didn't have a clue what 'Google was. "Did you know, by the way, that back in 600 BC," said the King "the Romans were the first to really make use of concrete? Apparently it was a clever mix of lime, volcanic ash and seawater. Know that?" "No sir, I wasn't aware of it. Jolly interesting though," said the Wing Commander. The King smiled and continued, "Yes, apparently those Roman chaps built all of their sea walls out of concrete and do you know, they're still there some 2,000 years later. Damned clever, what!" "Clever indeed, your Majesty. Ah, there we are, sir, over at two o'clock, it's the Haile Sand Fort," said the Wing Commander, pointing towards the Fort. "Magnificent! Don't suppose that the Fort will be here in another hundred or so years," said the King.

Back in the main cabin of the helicopter, the Queen was having an animated conversation with the Squadron Leader, and much to his surprise he discovered that she was very easy to talk to, both relaxed and charming. She said, "You know, Squadron Leader, a friend of mine was saying that the first sign of old age is when you go into a café and ask for a four minute boiled egg – and they ask you to pay up front!" As they were both laughing, she wriggled her toes in her slippers, "What a bloody relief it is to get those instruments of torture orft!" she said, pointing at her expensive shoes, "One's feet are throbbing and look like bloody Cornish Pasties!"

As they were chatting, the Squadron Leader's hand unconsciously slid down the side of the seat and much to his surprise he came across the small metal case that had been tucked away there by Major O'Brien. "Oh, something's slipped out of His Majesty's pocket," he thought, "better return it to him in case he needs it."

He grabbed hold of the case, then unbuckled his seat belt and said, "Would you excuse me for a moment, Ma'am, I just need to pop up to the flight deck." The Queen smiled and nodded, "You crack on, Squadron Leader," she said, reaching for a copy of that day's Hull Daily Mail, "I'll just see how 'Hull Tigers' got on yesterday. Prince James is an avid supporter and it'll give me something to talk to him about tonight."

"Excuse me Your Majesty, I think that this might have slipped out of your pocket?" Tony Whittingstall said to King George. The King smiled and turned to see what thc Squadron Leader was holding in his outstretched hand, then shook his head, "No, it's not mine, Squadron Leader. What is it?" As the King was speaking,

Whittingstall saw the small metal case starting to glow. It heated up very quickly, until it became too hot to hold. He gasped and dropped it onto the floor of the helicopter. As it hit the deck, there was a bright flash, followed by a thunderous, booming explosion, which blew the main door and windows off the chopper and hurtled the Squadron Leader back into the main compartment, landing at the feet of the shocked Queen.

The Wing Commander, who had been thrown forward and knocked unconscious by the force of the blast, was completely out of it and had slumped forward against the dual joy stick of the now badly damaged helicopter. The Sikorski promptly went into an uncontrolled tail spin and began fluttering down out of the sky like a falling leaf. The shocked King, who had been deafened by the blast but was still fully conscious, promptly reached forward, pulled the Wing Commander back off the joystick and then took control of the aircraft himself, before turning to the Queen and bellowing, "Margot! Brace! Brace! Brace for Collision!" "My handbag's just gone flying out of the bloody door, George! My God, what's happening, darling?" the Queen shouted.

As the King wrestled manfully with the controls, he saw that the helicopter, now barely under control, was on a direct collision course with the looming Fort, its grey reinforced concrete sidewalls sticking up out of the sea like an old fang, with Cleethorpes in the distance. "The bloody Fort, we're going to hit it!" the King shouted, "Damnation!"

The King's two dazed bodyguards looked on helplessly. There was absolutely nothing they could do to protect the Queen or the King under these circumstances, so they just clung on and waited for the inevitable collision and hoped that they would survive.

Despite being an excellent pilot there was very little that the King could do to stop the helicopter from colliding with the Fort. He would just have to go with the flow. The Wingco was still out cold, so couldn't help him. Giving it one more go, the King heaved back as hard as he could on the helicopter's joy stick and at the very last minute, much to his relief, he gradually regained a minimal amount of control of it, forcing the aircraft into the hover mode. Then, miraculously, the King managed to put the helicopter down on the very lip of the Fort's substantial battlements whilst doing his absolute best to keep it steady.

The King turned and shouted, "Everybody - off the chopper! Now! Hurry up - I can't hold her here for very much longer!" The Sikorski's engine was coughing and spluttering and belching out wreaths of black smoke which was beginning to filter into the passenger compartment.

The King's Personal Security Officer, Peter McGrath, staggered to his feet, unfastened the Queen's seatbelt and guided her out of the helicopter and safely onto the wide battlements, after which he returned to assist the other passengers to jump out of the helicopter and get down safely onto the Fort walkway. He shouted to the other Security Officer, "Look after the Queen,, stay with her, Tom!" He then ran back to the helicopter, climbed into the cockpit and unbuckled the unconscious Wing Commander, dragged him out of his seat and then passed him down to those still on the battlements. He then turned, intending to go back to help the King escape, but didn't make it in time.

Just as the helicopter's engine began to clatter, prior to failing completely, and looked as if it were about to fall off the battlements, the King turned and saw the Chief Inspector near the entrance to the helicopter, intending to climb back on board to help him. As the King wrestled valiantly to release his jammed safety harness, he shouted, "Never mind me, McGrath, I'll sort myself out! Go on, save yourself - that's an order!"

A furious Mr McGrath turned and sprinted away from the helicopter.

The King did his utmost to unfasten the buckle on his seat belt, cursing and wrestling furiously with it, but it had jammed and refused to release him. For some inexplicable reason it wasn't working, and now he was well and truly trapped in his seat. The helicopter was still teetering on the very edge of the battlements when its engine completely died, and without any warning the chopper suddenly tipped over the edge of the Fort and screeched noisily down the side of the reinforced concrete until slamming into the water, amazingly with its damaged rotor blades still slowly turning.

The last thing that the King remembered was the helicopter engine finally grinding to a halt and then the murky, freezing cold sea water creeping up inside the now silent cabin. He continued wrestling with the damaged seat belt buckle as the incoming water reached his heaving chest. "Shortest bloody reign ever!" he thought, as the Sikorski gave up the ghost and started to slip beneath the waves, the incoming water reaching the King's chin.

Arthur Palmer, an ancient lobster fisherman from Bridlington, well past retirement age, was returning to harbour after a very long day, with what he regarded as being very slim pickings. "Four chuffing lobsters and an Asda shopping trolley! How the bloody hell does a shopping trolley get this far out? It were 'ardly worth cranking th'engine up for," he grumbled to himself.

On hearing a loud explosion, he glanced up at the sky and saw to his horror that an obviously out of control helicopter seemed to be in big trouble. It was trailing smoke and spiralling down out of the sky like a falling leaf and heading straight towards a nearby Fort. "What the bloody 'ells going on there," muttered Arthur.

He scrabbled around for the hand mike attached to his radio set and called up the Coast Guard to report what he was watching. "Mayday! Mayday! Mayday! This is Arthur Palmer from the 'Salty Seagull' out of Bridlington! Come on you buggers! Answer me! Mayday! Mayday!"

As Arthur waited for the local Coastguard to respond, he watched in amazement as the helicopter gave a final heart stopping lurch then miraculously landed on the battlements at the top of the Napoleonic Fort, where it balanced precariously, smoke pouring from its rear compartment. He watched as several passengers jumped from inside the helicopter and onto the battlements, then ran off into the Fort. Arthur looked on in with disbelief as the helicopter slowly lurched off the top of the Fort, then slid down the side of it before plunging into the Humber. "Oh dear, I hope the poor buggers all got off," thought Arthur.

He spun the wheel of his launch as fast as he could, turning his boat around and heading straight for the Fort. "If they didn't all get off and if anyone's lucky enough to have survived that bloody fall, which I doubt, I'd better go and see if I can pick 'em up!" He called out to the other member of his two-man crew, Steve Walton, "Steve, don't just stand there looking simple, you gormless fart, come and grab this mike and keep trying to raise the Coastguard!" "Right away, boss," said Steve, grabbing the mike. "Mayday! Mayday! Mayday! Is there anyone there?" shouted Steve. Arthur tutted, "Press the bloody switch on top of the mike, you tit, or they won't hear you! When they answer you, tell 'em what's happened and that we need some help!" bellowed Arthur. "I'll get the boat alongside the Fort asap."

CHAPTER FIVE

'THERE'S BEEN A TERRIBLE ACCIDENT'

The 'phone jangled in Peter O'Brien's office, startling him out of his reverie. He picked it up and said, "OC! Yes, what is it?" "Hi Peter, it's the Chief of Staff." "Hello, Colonel," replied an immediately alert Peter. "Peter, can you get your arse across to the Headquarters conference room, straight away, please. The Brigadier wants an immediate 'O' Group with all of the Heads of Sheds. I'm afraid that there's been a terrible accident!" "Oh dear, what sort of accident?" asked O'Brien. "Better keep this to yourself for now, mate, but apparently the King's chopper's gone down somewhere over the Humber Estuary."

O'Brien's mouth suddenly went very dry, "You what?" he exclaimed. "Yes, I know, it's shocking," said the Chief of Staff, "apparently the Coastguard's just been on the blower to E Flight Ops to warn them off. The Coastguard's despatched a couple of their launches to the area and the OC E Flight's sent two Search & Rescue choppers to the scene."

"What the hell happened?" asked O'Brien. "Well, as far as I can ascertain, a local lobster fisherman claims to have heard a loud explosion and then saw what we believe to be the King's Sikorski dropping down out of the sky, trailing smoke, before crash landing on top of one of those old Forts. Apparently the chopper had also disappeared off the RAF Radar at the same time, setting off alarm bells. I'll be able to tell you more once you get over here. Gotta go, mate, see you shortly!" The Chief of Staff terminated the call abruptly.

Major O'Brien's bowels had turned to ice. He slumped into his office chair. "An explosion," he thought, "what the hell's all that about!" He felt sick as he remembered slipping the small metal case down the side of the helicopter seat. "No, it couldn't have been that, surely?" he thought. The more he thought about it, though, the more he realised that he had been taken for a mug by the duplicitous Chinese Captain Weng Hang Soon, who had tricked him into placing the metal case on board the Royal helicopter. It didn't take the brains of an Archbishop to deduce that it was the metal case that had more than likely been the cause of the explosion.

He was mortified when he realised that not only was he more than complicit in the death of the King and Queen, but also the other poor souls on board the helicopter.

It was obvious that Weng had lied and used him, and now he was in very deep shit. "That little bastard, Weng!" thought O'Brien, "well, he's not going to get away with it!" Hurtling across his office, he grabbed his beret and ran outside the building, where he saw his driver, Corporal Thurling, stood at the side of his staff car, puffing away on a cigarette. "Put that bloody cig out and take me to the Armoury straight away!" he ordered. His driver replied, "Yes sir!" then after extinguishing his cigarette, jumped into the driving seat of the staff car and they sped off, heading for the Unit Armoury.

The Unit Armourer, Sergeant Jed Hartharn REME, (*Royal Electrical and Mechanical Engineers*), smiled when he saw the Major. "Hello sir, and what can we do for you today?" "I need my pistol and forty rounds of live ammunition, straight away please!" said Major

O'Brien. "Oh, you off to the pipe range then, sir?" asked the Sergeant. "Forgive me, but there isn't time for a lengthy discussion Sarn't H, just get me what I asked for, asap, right!" The Sergeant nodded, "Right away, sir," thinking to himself, "Bloody 'ell, who's pulled his bleedin' chain!"

A few minutes later Jed handed the cleared pistol over to the Major, along with a small box of ammunition, containing forty rounds. "If you could kindly put your autograph here please, sir" he said, passing O'Brien a clip board. Major O'Brien scribbled his signature onto the document that was fastened to it, then legged it swiftly out of the Armoury. "Something's not right here," thought the Sergeant, "I'd better ring the RQM, (*Regimental Quartermaster*) and tell him. He'll know what to do, he always does."

"Take me over to the Officers' Mess!" O'Brien said to his driver, "and get your bloody clog down!" By the time he'd reached the Officers' Mess, the seething Major O'Brien had opened the box of ammunition and loaded his pistol. His driver, who had been watching him closely in the driving mirror, asked him, "Is everything OK, sir?" "Yes, why wouldn't it be, Thurling!" came the snarled reply, "Just shut up and drive!"

As soon as they reached the Officer's Mess, Major O'Brien jumped out of the staff car and dashed up to Captain Weng Hang Soon's room. He didn't pause to knock, but just kicked it open, smashing the lock and splintering the framework, and shouted, "Right, you little sh….." but the room was empty. He turned and hurtled downstairs to the Mess Manager's office. "Mr Raglan, have you seen Captain Weng Hang Soon?" "Sir, excuse me, but would you mind not waving that pistol in my face," said a very twitchy Mr Raglan. "Oh, sorry," said Major O'Brien, "Captain Weng?" "He left here about an hour ago, sir, told me that he was going down to Hull Paragon Station to catch the train to London."

"Did he say why he was going to London?" "No sir, he didn't, but he left here pretty sharpish I can tell you that much. I had to call the Guardroom and get the Duty Driver to come and drive him to the railway station. Yes, he was in a bit of a lickety-split was the Captain. There's skid marks on the tarmac outside the front door of the Mess."

The Officers' Mess Manager, Mr Bert Raglan glanced up at the clock on his office wall and said, "His train should be leaving Hull in about thirty minutes, sir. Is there a problem?" "Oh shit!" said O'Brien, then turned and ran out of the office. "I'd better give the Chief of Staff a call. Something's not right here," thought a puzzled Mr Raglan, "if you ask me, Major O'Brien's not firing on all cylinders, and he's waving that bloody pistol about as if he's Clint Eastwood!'

When he got back to his staff car, Major O'Brien snarled, "Is the Disco fully juiced up, Thurling?" His driver nodded, "Yes, of course, sir, always is, sir!" "Right, well take me straight down to Hull Railway Station - and get the pedal to the metal. You have my authority to break every speed rule in the book. Any comeback and it's down to me!" "You'd be much better getting a train from Beverley sir, they're every twenty minutes," said his driver, trying to be helpful. "Don't bloody argue man! Just do it!" shouted O'Brien.

Whilst Major O'Brien's staff car was hurtling along the Beverley by-pass, heading towards Hull Paragon Railway Station, Captain Weng was sat sipping a gin and tonic on board the Sabre Airlines Inter-City flight which was speeding along the runway and about to lift off from Humberside Airport, heading for London's Gatwick Airport. On reaching London, Weng would report directly to his contact at the Chinese Embassy in Portland Square, whom he had pre-warned to arrange a passport and get a suitable disguise ready for him, then book him onto a Shanghai Airlines flight from Heathrow Airport which would fly him on to Beijing's Capital Airport, taking him well out of harm's way. As an additional safety measure, he had also been granted diplomatic immunity by the Chinese Ambassador so that he could ease his way through Heathrow Airport without any formalities or fuss.

Major O'Brien sprinted onto the platform at Hull Paragon Railway Station and saw that apart from a train leaving Platform One, the station was completely devoid of trains. Spotting a member of staff meandering about the empty platform he called out, "You there! That train that's just left, was that the train for London?"

The man shook his head and replied, "No mate. That one's empty, it's terminating at Goole sidings. There's no more trains going from here today. Don't you read the papers, there's a one day strike on, nothing's moving!" "Including you," thought the irate Major.

"Oh bollocks!" said a furious O'Brien, "What about National Express buses then? They go from here don't they?" "The National Express bus for London left here at 8 o'clock this morning, boss. There won't be another one now until tomorrow morning. The only way you'll get to London today is to drive yourself down there or thumb a lift!"

Without pausing to reply, a furious O'Brien turned and stomped off the platform. "Bloody Ruperts, think they own the place," mumbled the staff member, "Huh, I had to put up with that sort of crap when I was in the Territorials (*Reserve Army*), but not anymore." He defiantly stuck up two fingers at the departing Major and called out, but not too loudly, "Get stuffed!"

Back on the Beverley by-pass, on the return journey to Leconfield, Major O'Brien was slumped in the passenger seat of his staff car, utterly morose and deep in thought.

Suddenly he sat up, startling his driver, "Of course!" he said, "Turn this bloody thing around and take me to Humberside Airport, Thurling!"

"Humberside Airport sir?" "Yes! Do you have to repeat everything I say?" "Repeat everything you say? No sir! Humberside Airport it is, sir." said Thurling, "Oh sir, by the way, I'm afraid I haven't got any cash on me to pay the Humber Bridge toll."

"Don't worry about that, man. I'll use my credit card. Get your bloody clog down!" ordered O'Brien.

CHAPTER SIX

'THE TAILOR'S DUMMY'

Yorkshireman, Dan Clayton, gave a frustrated, heartfelt sigh then switched his non-bleeping metal detector off. "That's enough for today," he thought. Dan and his wife Steph, both of them literally long-standing, enthusiastic metal detectorists, had been scouring the beach at Hornsea since that morning's tide had gone out. They'd found a few low denomination modern day coins dropped by careless holiday makers, an unusual bottle top and a child's bracelet, but nothing of any real value. He called out to Steph, "Hey Steph, I think we'd better call it a day, the tide's starting to come back in," Steph shouted back, "OK!" then a moment later she shouted, "Dan, look, over there - what's that bobbing around at the water's edge, looks like a tailor's dummy!"

Dan looked across to where she was pointing, "It'll be summat and now't," he said, "I'll go and have a look though, just to make sure. You never know." "I'll wait over here if you don't mind," said Steph. The 'dummy' was rolling gently from side to side, in time with the lapping incoming waves.

Dan walked across the sand towards the object and saw straight away that it wasn't a tailor's dummy. As he got closer he could see what looked like a male body. Mystified, he thought, "My God, I think it's a stiff! I wonder if it's someone who's fallen off a ship or maybe one of those unfortunate boat people?" He knelt down to examine the man's body. The man was wearing what had clearly been a very expensive pin-striped suit, had socks on but no shoes. As he was dragging the man out of the rolling surf, the man suddenly gasped, coughed up some sea water and opened his eyes, scaring Dan witless.

"Jesus Christ!" exclaimed Dan, nearly dropping the man back into the water. The man looked up at him and whispered, "Oh, hello, have you come to help me?" then lapsed back into unconsciousness. Turning towards Steph, Dan shouted, "Come over here and give me a hand, Steph. It's not a dummy, it's a bloke - and he's still breathing!"

Dragging the man out of the surf and onto dry sand, Dan took his own jacket off, rolled it up and placed it beneath the man's head. "Just catch your breath, mate, and then we'll see about getting you some help," he said, gently patting the man's cheek. The man's eyes fluttered open again, he nodded, tried to smile, then his head lolled forwards and he slid back into unconsciousness. Dan noticed that the man's head, face and hands had taken a bit of a battering and so had his nose, which had a small cut and a distinct kink in it. "You've really been in the wars, old pal," murmured Dan.

As Steph arrived and saw the state the man was in, she gasped and asked Dan, "What's happened to him?" "I dunno love," said Dan, "he was conscious a few seconds ago, but he's back in the 'Land of Nod' now, so I didn't get chance to question him properly."

Steph looked around at the now empty beach, "Well, there's no-one around here to help us, everyone's buggered off home. What are we going to do with him then?" she asked, nodding towards the man. "Well, we can't leave him here can we, the tide's coming in, so we'd better carry him off the beach and over to the camper van. It should be OK to do that, most of his injuries seem to be on his head and hands. There's no blood or broken bones anywhere else as far as I can tell, I've just given him the once over. So, you grab his legs and I'll get his arms. Come on! One, two, three!"

As they lifted the man up from the sand and began carrying him over towards their camper van, he moaned and began mumbling. "What's he saying?" asked Steph. "I can't be sure for certain," replied Dan, "but I think he's speaking in English. Come on, let's get him into the van!"

They carried the man's limp body across to their ancient, much-loved Volkswagen camper van, which was tucked away in the car park at the rear of Hornsea Floral Hall, immediately adjacent to the beach. Lifting him on board the camper van, they heaved him onto the side couch, removed his soaking suit then dried him off as best they could. Steph dabbed at his superficial wounds with a piece of kitchen towel soaked in Dettol disinfectant and then stuck a blue sticking plaster across the bridge of his apparently broken nose.

"That'll have to do him until we can get someone to have a proper look at him," said Steph. Dan replied, "Better get a pot of Yorkshire tea organised, Steph, that might help to revive him a bit. Plenty of sugar for energy!" Steph nodded, "Aye, and then he might be able to tell us what's happened to him." As they were talking, the man's eyes flickered open again and he started mumbling something unintelligible. "Ah, he's back in the land of the living," said Steph, "I'll go and put the kettle on."

Dan sat on the side of the bed, holding and gently patting the back of the man's hand, "Now then, old lad, looks like you've really been in the wars, but you're safe now. Er, you do speak English don't you?"

The man nodded and replied, "Yes, I certainly do - and French and German - I think." "We'll make do with English just for now," said Dan. The man tried to sit up, but Dan restrained him, "No, no, you just lie there and take things easy for a while. There's a nice reviving cup of tea on its way to you." said Dan.

"Er, where am I?" asked the man, looking around the van, "and what am I doing here?" "Listen, chum," said Dan, "we'll sort all that out later. We, that's my wife Steph and me, found you unconscious on the Hornsea beach. We were out there doing a bit of metal detecting. Looks like you've been bashed about a bit - banged your head, damaged your hands and I think that you might have broken your nose, so you're obviously a bit confused at the moment. We should really be getting you to a hospital and have you examined properly by a Doctor."

The man shook his head, sighed and replied, "No, no hospitals. It's just a few scratches, that's all. I've had worse injuries on the Polo field! I, I just need to gather my thoughts, and then I'm sure that everything will be tickety-boo."

Steph arrived with a steaming mug of tea, "Here you are love, the mug that cheers. Help him to sit up Dan, put some of those cushions behind his back. Can you manage a couple of shortbread biscuits, love?" she asked the man. He smiled and nodded, "Ah, shortbread - my favourites! Thank you dear lady, that would be quite lovely."

Dan held the mug up to the man's lips and helped him to take a sip of the hot, sweet tea. Steph passed him the partially opened packet of biscuits. The man extracted a biscuit from the packet and examined it closely before nibbling the edge of it, "Oh, I see that they're Highgrove Organics! Splendid!" he said. Steph nodded,

"Yes, you can buy them locally now. They're a bit posh, but there's a special offer on at the 'Pound Shop' this week, two for the price of one, so I thought that we'd treat ourselves to a couple of packets." "Jolly good show!" said the man.

Steph drew Dan to one side, "Hey, Dan, he sounds a bit posh don't you think. You know what, I'll bet a pound to a pinch of the other that he's slipped and fallen off one of those flash yachts that park up in Bridlington Harbour, and that the tide's washed him around here to Hornsea." Dan nodded in agreement, "Maybe so. Either way, he's been lucky to survive. Well, we'll let him finish his tea and biscuits and despite what he says, we'll drive him across to the A & E (*Accident and Emergency*) department at the Princess Diana Hospital in Grimsby and get them to give him the once over." At the mention of Princess Diana, the man turned towards them and smiled wanly.

"You'd better dig out one of your spare shell suits and lend it to him then," said Steph, "his suit's bogging. It'll definitely need dry cleaning to get rid of the salt. We can't let him go wandering around the hospital wrapped in one of our threadbare travel blankets and wearing a pair of soaking wet shreddies. Oh, and you'd better ask him what shoe size he is. He can't go padding around in his bare feet either. You can loan him a pair of your crocs!"

"You know, Steph, there's summat not quite right here," said a puzzled Dan. "What do you mean?" she asked. "I mean, why would someone who's out yachting be wearing a posh suit?" he said. Steph shrugged, "Perhaps he was going somewhere, or had just come back?"

Turning to the man, Dan said, "When you've finished your cuppa, my friend, I know that you're not keen, but we're going to take you straight to the local A & E Department and get you checked over. That OK?" As the man nodded, Steph dabbed gently at the man's nose with a clean handkerchief, making him wince. He said, "I don't suppose that I have any option, but thank you very much anyway, you're so very kind." "No problem, dear," said Steph, "I'm sure that you'd do the same for us. We'd call an ambulance, but they're on strike again." The man sighed and nodded.

Dan asked him, "So, what's your name then, have you remembered?" The man thought for a moment then said, "Do you know, for the life me, I can't recall." "So you don't know how you came to fall into the sea then?" The man shook his head and winced, "No, I'm afraid not. It's all a complete blank." "That'll probably be a bit of concussion," said Steph, "here, let me chuck another blanket over you, you're shivering, you poor thing. Don't be so tight, give him another biscuit, Dan."

After the man had been checked out at the hospital's A & E, he was classified by the Duty Doctor as being 'Walking Wounded' and promptly discharged because there was a serious shortage of beds and they were needed for more serious cases. The Medics had confirmed that the man was indeed suffering from a mild concussion and that his other cuts and bruises weren't particularly serious. His broken nose was strapped up with a more substantial piece of sticking plaster and he was told that he just needed a bit of bed rest, then things, like the return of his memory, would resolve themselves in due course.

"Bloody useless," said Steph, as they walked back to their camper van with the man. "I could've diagnosed all of that stuff my pigging self!" "At least he's had a couple of X-Rays and a scan - and they've taped his conk up properly," said Dan, "He looked like Adam Ant with that blue sticking plaster you put on his conk." "It's all I could find in the first aid box," said Steph defensively.

"So, what the hell are we supposed to do with him now?" she asked Dan. "Well, we can't just dump him here in the hospital car park and leave him, can we. Suppose I'd better call the cops and ask them what we should with him," said Dan. "No, I've got a better idea, let's take him home with us. We don't want to be sat in this car park all day waiting for a police car to turn up. At least we can give him a hot meal and the police can come and interview him there in comfortable surroundings," said Steph.

They clambered back on board their camper van. The man suddenly brightened up and said, "That's it! George!" then slumped into a chair and promptly fell asleep. "Look at the poor bugger, he's drifted off already. Absolutely cream crackered. Come on, let's lift him out of that chair and put him onto the bed, he's out cold," said Steph. "That'll be those tablets the Doc gave him," said Dan, "He said that they were strong enough to stun a bull moose!"

They lifted the man onto the bed and covered him over with a blanket. Dan went and sat in the driving seat of the camper van and started the engine up. "OK, we'll head back home and sort things out from there then. Oh, and we can call in at Whiteheads chippie on our way back to Beverley," said Dan. "I'll switch the van's oven on, then that'll keep the food warm until we get home," said Steph. She shook her head, "What a strange old day this is turning out to be. We're out there on the beach all day and nothing happens, then we stumble across the 'Man Who Never Was' and we're taking him back home to Beverley with us!" Dan nodded, "Aye, we've found some strange things when we've been out metal detecting, but a 'bod' – that's definitely a first!"

CHAPTER SEVEN

' THE KING IS DEAD –
LONG LIVE THE KING! '

There was a gentle tap on the door. Prince James called out, "Enter!" He smiled when he saw that it was his Equerry, Major Richard De Vere Pilkington-Manston. "Dickie, my dear chap, I didn't expect to see you here until after Tiffin." "Sorry to intrude, but I need to have a word with you immediately, Your Majesty," said Richard.

James looked puzzled, "Did you forget yourself and just say, 'Your Majesty' Dickie?" he asked. Highly emotional and very near to tears, Richard nodded and replied, "I wonder, sir, forgive me - sire, if we could have a word away from the youngsters," glancing at James' children. James nodded and said, "Of course. Er, Penny, would you excuse us for a moment, I'm just popping outside to have a quick word with Dickie." "Hi Dickie!" said a smiling Princess Penelope. Bobbing his head, Dickie replied, "Ma'am."

"So, Dickie, what the hell's going on?" asked Prince James. "Well, sire," said Richard, "It grieves me to have to tell you this, but earlier on this afternoon, His Majesty, accompanied by Her Majesty, lifted off from the Army base at Leconfield, East Yorkshire, in the Sikorski and headed out over the Humber Estuary. Apparently the King wanted to have a quick scoot around an old Fort on the way home." "And did you say that Her Majesty was accompanying him?" asked James. "Yes, I'm afraid so, sir, sire." "You say 'afraid so.' That sounds a little ominous." "Better brace yourself for some very bad news, sire. It appears that there was an explosion on board and the helicopter was fatally damaged, although most of those on board survived. Sadly, His Majesty the King went down with the ship, as it were."

"Saints preserve us!" gasped a shocked James, "Who else was travelling on the chopper?" Richard glanced at the piece of paper he was clutching in his hand - "There was Her Majesty the Queen, Adrian Longman, the King's Equerry, Lady Sara Langthorne, the Queen's Companion, two Special Branch officers and two RAF chaps, the pilot and co-pilot. "My God," said James, " you said bomb, Dickie. So do we know what happened yet?"

"Not really, they're still trying to sort it all out, Your Royal High, er, Your Majesty, but apparently a 'Mayday' call was received from a local fisherman, which has now been confirmed by the RAF and the RNLI, reporting that he'd heard an explosion and saw that a helicopter was in trouble - that would be the Sikorski as there were no other helicopters in the area. Then, as the Sikorski approached the old Fort, the fisherman heard a smaller explosion and when he looked up he saw the chopper, trailing smoke, falling towards the water, before miraculously, and right at the very last minute, managing to put down on the battlements of the Fort. By the grace of God, the passengers, including Her Majesty, managed to evacuate the aircraft, just before it rolled off the battlements and fell down into the Humber then sank. Unfortunately, the King was still on board. Apparently he was trapped by his seat belt."

"And His Majesty, Dickie, I presume from what you're telling me, didn't survive the fall?" asked a shocked James.

Richard shook his head, "Apparently not, sire. Having said that, as His Majesty's remains, forgive me, have not yet been recovered, we are not one hundred per cent certain that he is lost, but it is doubted that he would have survived the fall, let alone anything else. The others who were travelling with him on board the aircraft, including Her Majesty, were rescued from the Fort and brought safely back to shore. Once they've been checked over by the Medics, they'll be flown straight back to London. The Secretary of State for Defence has sent his private jet to Humberside Airport to collect them. As we speak, there are Royal Marine specialist divers and RAF Search and Rescue people out at the Fort combing the area diligently. They haven't managed to locate any helicopter wreckage as yet though."

"So there's a faint chance that the King could still be alive then, Dickie?" James asked, hopefully. Richard shook his head, "It seems highly unlikely, sire. It is doubtful that anyone would have survived a crash as serious as that. Apparently the helicopter was very badly damaged when it hit the water and sank."

"So where does that leave us then?" asked James. "In the first instance, I regret to say that as a direct consequence of this most regrettable accident, if indeed it was an accident, it means that you are now the rightful King, Your Majesty."

Richard stood up and bowed, "regrettably, someone has to say it first, I suppose - 'The King is Dead! God save the King!" "My God!" said James, his face turning ashen, as the enormity of what he'd been told sank in, and he realised the full consequences of the helicopter crash.

The room door was flung open and a smiling Princess Penelope came bouncing into the room, full of the joys of Spring. She said to James, "Jimmy-Jams, are you joining us for Tiffin? Come on! Cook's made some of your favourite 'Jammy Dodgers.' There's enough for you too, Dickie, if you want to come and join us!'" Seeing James' drawn face, and Richard dabbing the tears from his eyes, she immediately sensed that something was badly amiss, and the smile fell from her face.

Prince James patted the seat beside him, "You'd better come and sit down beside me, darling. I have something truly terrible to tell you," he said. The Princess shook her head and tutted, "Oh no, it's not your brother playing silly sods again is it?" "No, my darling, not this time. It's something far worse than that. Do come and sit down."

Once James had explained to Penelope what had happened, and that he was now King, and she was destined to be Queen much sooner than expected, she gasped with shock, then burst into floods of tears.

As James put his arm around her trembling shoulders, she whispered, "My God, James, Papa, the King gone! I can't believe it! Poor Margaret, how must she be feeling. We must call her straight away." James turned to Richard, "Can you get that organised please, Dickie" Richard nodded, "Of course, Your Majesty." Penelope sobbed. "What are we going to do now, we're not really ready for any of this, James. My God, how are we going to explain it to the children?" "You'd better leave that to me, darling Penny. Remember, I had counselling training in that sort of thing when I was in the Army," said James.

CHAPTER EIGHT

'GOLDEN SCRAPS'

"Sither, would you like some of this HP relish on your fish and chips, lad?" asked Steph. The man nodded and replied, "Oh, yes please, that would be rather lovely, I'm starving. Er, forgive me asking, but what's this little pile of crispy golden thingummy bobs, right next to the fried fish?" Steph smiled, "Them there?" she asked, pointing. He nodded, "Yes, er, them there." She said, "They're called 'scraps.' You never had 'em before?" The man shook his head, "Er, I don't believe so." "Well," said Steph, "you don't know what you've been missing, lad. They're a Yorkshire delicacy are scraps. They're our version of caviar! They've even started selling scraps in sexy little boxes in Marks and Sparks, would you believe! Go on, give them a good larruping of salt and malt vinegar and get stuck in before they get cold. By the way, have you remembered who you are yet, love?" she asked as she poured him a mug of tea.

He shook his head. "I think that I very nearly did just then, but it wouldn't quite surface." "Never mind, love, I'm sure it will in due course. Take your time, there's no real rush is there, but we'll have to find out soon 'cos someone will be looking for you," said Steph, passing him the tea. "Tell you what, I'll just switch the telly on - it's time for the evening news. We can see what's going on in the world."

She called out, "Dan! Come and get your fish and chips before they get cold. I've just put the news on!" "I was getting some more bread and butter," said Dan, "our guests eaten nearly half a loaf." As they sat there tucking into their fish and chips, the TV screen dimmed briefly and the National Anthem was played prior to the news coming on. Suddenly a sombre photograph of King George the Seventh appeared. "Hello, what's going on here then? Something's happened." said Dan.

The soberly dressed newsreader came into vision and announced that His Majesty the King's Sikorski helicopter had suffered some sort of engine failure whilst he was on board and as a result it had crashed into the Humber Estuary. It was believed that most of the crew and passengers had survived, including the Queen who was travelling with the King at the time. The King, however, who had been on a visit to the Defence

School of Transportation at nearby Leconfield earlier in the afternoon, appeared to have been lost at sea, although a thorough search was being conducted in the area. Steph's jaw dropped, "My God, what's going on! I can't believe it. The King gone, just like that!" she said, crunching on her scraps. "It'll be those bloody foreign terrorists!" said Dan. "The swine's!" replied Steph.

The man dropped his knife and fork down onto his plate with a clatter, startling everyone, and then murmured, "My God, I think that I've just remembered who I am!" Not hearing what he'd whispered, Steph said, "Shush dear, let's watch the news. This is history in the making. More tea?" The man nodded. "Er, don't you want those scraps?" Dan asked him. The man shook his head, "No, not really, thank you." "Pass 'em over here then, lad. Waste not, want not, eh!"

After the news had finished, Steph reached forward and switched the TV off. "Well, that's a turn up for the books. Poor old King George. I liked him as well. Now then, did you say something, love?" she asked the man. He nodded, "Yes, I think that I've remembered who I am." "Oh, that's nice – so, who are you then?" "Well, I do believe that I'm King George the Seventh!"

Dan smiled at him, "Yes, and I'm Sir Elton John! Now come on, chum, you can't be the King can you. You've just watched the news - the King, I'm afraid, seems to have docked his clogs in the Humber!"

George shook his head, "No, he hasn't - I mean, no I haven't. I'm not dead. I am alive and kicking! Yes, it's all coming back to me now. I had to make an emergency landing on that Fort in the Humber. Something had gone wrong on board the chopper and I had to take over from the pilot who was badly injured. The RAF Wingco who normally pilots it was out like a light, you see. Luckily, I was sat next to him and took control of the helicopter. Eventually, after a monumental struggle, I managed to get the failing chopper to hover just above the battlements of the Fort until the passengers had deplaned, including Her Majesty thank God, then the engine finally conked out and my helicopter rolled down the side of the Fort and into the Humber. Yes, that's it!"

He continued, "When the chopper hit the water, I remember struggling to release my seatbelt and then wriggling out of the water-filled cabin. As I exited the aircraft, something hit me on the back of the head, probably a rotor blade. Yes, it's all coming back to me now. There was some sort of explosion on board the aircraft." "What, you mean like a bomb going off?" asked Steph. The man nodded, "Yes, I'm sure that's what it was. There was this bloody great bang before all hell broke loose and we lost power. Luckily, the rotor blades kept turning at a fair lick until just before we fell off the side of the Fort. Kept us balanced for a while, don't you see. They slowed right down once we hit the water though." "Luckily for you if that's what cracked you on the back of your bonce," said Steph.

Steph and Dan looked at each other, then after a moment's pause, Steph murmured, "If he is who he says he is, what the chuffing hell do we do now then?" Dan replied, "Well, I suppose that we'd better give the authorities a call and have his story checked out. It seems a bit far-fetched to me, but you never know." Turning to the King, he said, "Are you sure that you're the King. You don't look a bit like him." The King smiled, "Well, I have been knocked about a bit and my face is rather swollen." Steph stared at him, then after a moment she jumped to her feet and did a sweeping curtsey.

"What are you doing, Steph?" said Dan. "Dan - he's right, he is the King. You've only got to look at his eyes and listen to him speak. My God we've been thick! We should have guessed it before now," said Steph. "just have a look at that signet ring he keeps twiddling," she said. "What about it?" Dan asked her. "Look - it's got the Prince of Wales feathers engraved on it," she replied. Dan glanced across and examined the ring. His jaw dropped. He leapt to his feet and bowed, "Sir, why didn't you tell us all this stuff when we found you on the beach?" "Because I was confused, didn't bloody well know my arse from my elbow, did I!" replied King George, scooping up a few chips. "I say, these are jolly tasty," he said.

"So what do we do next then? Who should we call to let them know that you're safe and sound?" Dan asked the King. "Please don't do anything precipitate, I beg of you, " said the King. "I don't even know what precipitate means," said Dan. "In essence, it means 'Stand Slack' for the moment," said George, "I'd just like a little bit more time to clear my head and think things through."

"What do you need to think about?" Steph asked him, "You're the King, you've survived the crash, thank God, and now it's time that your people came and got you. You don't belong in a three up, three down house in Butterfly Meadows, Beverley, do you. Oh, your family will be so relieved."

The King looked immensely sad, "I can't believe what's happened. I do hope that my darling Margaret is unharmed." "Well, they said on the news that she'd been rescued, so I don't think that you need to worry about her, I mean Her Majesty," said Steph, "Tell you what, I'll put the kettle on and make a fresh pot of tea whilst you and my Dan here talk things through. It's all beyond me is this." She picked up the empty plates and the tea tray and carried them into the kitchen, leaving the King and Dan to talk. "I'd have used my best Doulton if I'd known it was him," she thought.

Later, when the exhausted King, who had drifted off, was snoozing in an armchair, and Steph was tidying up, Dan said, "Well, I don't care what he says, I'm going to 'phone the Army base at Leconfield. They'll know what to do with him. We can't have the King sat there in our front room, kipping after scoffing fish and chips, when everyone's out there on the Humber searching for him. It's ridiculous." "Let me do it, I'm much better at these things than you are," said Steph, "you'll only balls things up."

She reached into her handbag and pulled out her cell 'phone, then tapped a number into it. When someone answered, she asked, "Operator, can you give me the telephone number of the Leconfield Army base please. Yes, that's right, the Leconfield Army base. I need to speak to their Duty Officer or someone important, as a matter of great urgency. You'll put me through will you. Yes, I'll hold. Thank you very much."

CHAPTER NINE

'IT'S JUST ANOTHER NUT JOB'

"Brigadier," said Lieutenant Colonel Lacy, the Brigadier looked up, "Yes, what is it, Sean?" "I've just had a call from the Duty Officer at the Guardroom, seems that they've just had a 'phone call from some old biddy living in Beverley who claims that the King is sat in her front room eating fish and chips." The Brigadier sighed, "Another bloody nut job! That's the third today! As if we haven't got enough to worry about. Have we kept the Blue Jobs (*RAF*) up to speed? The Chief of Staff nodded, "Yes, Brigadier." "And what are they doing about it?" "They've sent someone down to Beverley to investigate." "Complete bloody waste of time," said the Brigadier. "Should we stand the Search Teams out at the Fort down, sir?" The Brigadier shook his head, "No, not yet. They must keep searching until they find what's left of that damned helicopter. It'll be dark soon and that'll only add to our problems. Incidentally, anything on Major O'Brien yet?" The Chief of Staff shook his head, "Nothing at all, Brigadier. Oh, hang on a moment, sir, that's my 'phone ringing. I'd better go and see who it is."

A few minutes later a worried looking Chief of Staff returned. "Well?" asked the Brigadier. "Major O'Brien's driver, Corporal Thurling, has just rung the Guardroom from Paragon Railway Station in Hull." "What the blazes is he doing down there?" asked the irritated Brigadier. "Apparently, sir, Major O'Brien ordered him to drive down to the railway station to see if they could find Captain Weng." "Captain Weng the Chinese Army guy? What the bloody hell has he got to do with any of this?"

The Chief of Staff shook his head, "No idea yet, Brigadier. I'll try and find out though. Anyway, it appears that by the time O'Brien reached the railway station, Captain Weng had left for London on the train, so Major O'Brien jumped into the Disco, leaving his driver stood at the entrance to the station and then drove off at a rate of knots, shouting at the driver to catch a bus back to Leconfield and that he was heading for London to find Weng."

The Brigadier sighed, "I don't suppose that he left his pistol with the Driver, did he - that would be too much to ask?" The Chief of Staff shook his head "No sir, I'm afraid that he's still got it with him - that and a box of ammo. The good news though, Brigadier, is that the Armourer got confused and issued O'Brien with blank rounds instead of live ones. The one's that we use for sporting events." "Thank God for small mercies! Has the Regimental Quartermaster confirmed that?" asked the Brigadier. The Chief of Staff nodded, "Yes sir, that was the RQM on the dog and bone just now."

"Bloody hell, you couldn't write this. It's like a damned Whitehall farce!" said the Brigadier, his luxuriant moustache twitching. "Well, we can't be held responsible if Major O'Brien's gone rogue, sir," said the Chief of Staff. "Gone rogue! Don't be so damned silly, Sean," said the Brigadier, "he's not a bloody African elephant. The man's obviously experiencing some sort of mental crisis. He should never have been posted to DST in the first place, we haven't got the facilities for that sort of thing here and you certainly can't rely on the NHS. He should have been sent directly to the Depot." The Chief of Staff nodded, "Totally agree with you, sir."

The Brigadier sighed, " Suppose that I'd better give HQ 2 Div (*Headquarters 2ⁿᵈ Division*) at York a call and let the GOC's (*General Officer Commanding*) man know what's going on before the General sees or hears something in or on the Media. This is going to send him off on one."

"With respect, a word of caution, Brigadier," said the Chief of Staff, "Might it not be worth waiting for just a little while longer until the situation becomes a tad clearer? That way we might have something more positive to tell the General."

The Brigadier shook his head, "No. I'd rather the General didn't hear about any of this on BBC TV's 'Look North' or something. You know how volatile he can be." "Suppose you're right, sir, but might I suggest that you have a quick word with the Chief Constable before you do ring the GOC's office? Maybe the Police can mount road blocks and have O'Brien stopped, arrested and brought back here?" The Brigadier nodded, "Yes, that's a spiffing idea, Sean. Good bit of arse-covering material there, what! Better get me O'Brien's vehicle details and I'll give Sir Michael a tinkle right now."

The Brigadier gave a long drawn out sigh, "I was at school with him you know." "What, Major O'Brien, sir?" replied the Chief of Staff brightly. "No, you bloody nincompoop - the Chief Constable, Mike Fraser!" "I'll go and get you

O'Brien's vehicle details, sir," said the Chief of Staff, fleeing from the Brigadier's office before he dug himself into an even deeper hole.

The Brigadier picked up his 'phone and tapped in the Chief Constable's contact number. After a few rings, Sir Michael answered personally. "Mike? Hello, it's Peter Chambers-Renton over at Leconfield. Look, I need your help, old chum. I suppose you'll have been told about the telephone call from the nut-job over here in Beverley by now, the one saying that King George is sat in her front room scoffing a plate of fish and chips. You have, eh. Good. Well, actually I'm not ringing you about that in the first instance. You see, as if losing the King wasn't bad enough, I've also got another serious problem. You see, just over an hour ago one of my officers, a Major, for some reason has thrown his 'Teddy' out of the pram and legged it in one of our vehicles, and here's the kicker, he's carrying a Sigsauer 9 mil pistol and some ammunition - blanks, fortunately, although that's bad enough. I'd like your lads to try and help apprehend him."

As the Brigadier was chatting to the Chief Constable, the Chief of Staff returned to the office and slid a piece of paper in front of the Brigadier on which was pencilled O'Brien's vehicle details. "Yes, I've got the vehicle registration details right here, Mike. It's a black Land Rover Discovery, registration 'Romeo Niner Niner, Tango Echo X-Ray. Perhaps you could feed that into your ANPRS (*Automatic Number Plate Recognition System*) or whatever it is that you chaps do, and see if we can stop and lift him without any dramas?" He paused waiting for the Chief Constable's reply. "No, I haven't got those particular details to hand. Just give me a couple of minutes and I'll get back to you, Mike." The Brigadier rang off.

Turning to his Chief of Staff, the Brigadier said, "Sean, get me the serial number of O'Brien's pistol from the Sergeant Hartharn, the Armourer will you. The Chief Constable wants to feed the information through to his Mobile Armed Response Team. Come on man, don't stand there gawping! Chop-chop!" "Right away, sir." said the harassed Chief of Staff, dashing back to his office. He returned a few minutes later and said, "The Sigsauer 9 mil pistol, Brigadier. Here's the serial number," he said, passing a slip of paper to the Brigadier.

Thundering down the crowded A1, Major O'Brien mumbled, "I'll bet that little shite-hawk Weng's heading for the safety of his Embassy and once he's there he'll probably claim Diplomatic Immunity. Well, that's not going to help him because I'm going in there either to arrest him or put a round through his head! No-one makes a fool of Peter O'Brien, only Peter O'Brien."

O'Brien had driven at great speed over to Humberside Airport from Hull's Paragon Railway Station, crashing through the Humber Bridge barriers along the way and causing traffic mayhem. Unfortunately, by the time he'd arrived at Humberside Airport he discovered that Captain Weng had left there half an hour previously on the daily inter-city flight to London.

Grinding his teeth furiously, an enraged O'Brien had sprinted back to his vehicle, jumped inside it and roared out of the airport, heading for Doncaster Railway Station, where he intended to board the very next train to Kings Cross in London. He was determined to catch up with Weng and deal with him, before Weng escaped and the trail got cold.

On reaching Doncaster Railway Station, O'Brien abandoned his vehicle in the car park and ran onto the main concourse of the station, where he spotted a Ticket Inspector. "You there!" he shouted. The startled Ticket Inspector turned and when he saw that he was being addressed by an Army officer, he glanced admiringly at the Major's DPM's (*Disruptive Pattern Material (Camouflage)*) uniform then sprang to attention and said, "Yizzah! How can I help you, sah?"

"When's the next train to London Kings Cross arrive?" asked O'Brien. "Well, you're lucky there, sir, there's a Virgin train due in, in fifteen minutes. Just time for you to grab a nice cup of char from the station buffet whilst you're waiting, eh sir! I'm picking up the train here myself. " "Thank you," said O'Brien, "and am I able to purchase a ticket on board the train or do I have to go to the booking office?" The Ticket Inspector nodded, "On the train will be OK, sir. I'll organise all that for you. I'll also find you a seat in First Class, you being a senior officer and all that."

"That's very kind of you, Mr.....?" replied O'Brien. The Ticket Inspector smiled, "Hepworth, sah, George Hepworth. I was in the h'Army myself, sir. I was a Master Chef in the ACC (*Army Catering Corps*) - that's how I know the tea's good here." "Thanks. I'd better go and get myself a mug then, Mr Hepworth," said O'Brien. "I'd advise you to keep an ear out for the announcements, sir. The train will arrive at Platform Four in approximately fifteen minutes, sir, and it's running on time. As I said, you need to listen for the announcement. It won't hang about once it's due to leave, I'll make sure of that." O'Brien nodded, said a brusque "Got it – cheers, Mr Hepworth!" and headed off for the station buffet.

"Chief Inspector? It's Sergeant Troth of the Metropolitan Central Division here, sir. Our Doncaster lads have stopped an Army vehicle, a Land Rover Discovery, registration number R 99 TEX, leaving the car park at Doncaster Railway Station. I've confirmed that it's the one we've all been searching for, but unfortunately the Major wasn't driving it, just some thieving little opportunist who found it doors open, keys still in the ignition and the engine running – a gift for the tealeaves around there apparently. He's had his collar felt. The locals sent a couple of their lads into the railway station to see if they can find out if anyone's seen the Army Major, or indeed if he's still lurking up there. They know that the Major is tooled up, so they're treading carefully"

Sergeant Troth listened for a moment, then said, "I agree with you wholeheartedly, sir, it's a right balls up." He tutted, "Typical bloody Army. They couldn't organise a piss up in a bleedin' brewery!"

CHAPTER TEN

'FAR FROM THE MADDING CROWD'

"Excuse me, sah, sorry to disturb you, but I just thought you'd like to know that we'll be pulling into King's Cross Station very shortly, sah," said the Ticket Inspector. "Oh, thanks very much for letting me know, Mr Hepworth," said Major O'Brien. "No problem, sah! I was just thinking, sah, if you'd like to accompany me when the train arrives on the platform, we middle-management employees have the use of our own side gate near the main exit, sort of a little perk, which you're welcome to use, sah. If you'd care to accompany me, you can slip through the gate it and it'll mean that you won't be jostled by the 'Maddening Crowd' and have to queue at the ticket barrier." "It's 'Madding Crowd,' you oaf," thought O'Brien. "Yes sir, it's one of the few perks that we have left these days. The taxi rank's just around the corner, unless you've got a staff car waiting to pick you up that is?"

O'Brien forced a smile, "No, no staff car I'm afraid. Defence cuts. I'll just jump into taxi, Mr

Hepworth - and thank you for all of your help. I'm very grateful." O'Brien took out his wallet and removed a crisp ten pound note, "Here you are, Mr Hepworth, get yourself a sippers, it's beer you chaps drink isn't it?" Hepworth smiled and nodded, "Yes sir, can't beat a nice drop of Taylor's Ales, eh." The tenner disappeared into his trouser pocket faster than you could say, 'Rishi Sunak.' "Again, thanks for your help, Mr Hepworth, much appreciated. Once I get back to my unit I'll drop a note to your Managing Director about how much you've gone out of your way to help me today." "That's very thoughtful of you, sir. We 'Squaddies' should stick together, eh! If you stay in your seat, I'll come and collect you once the train draws to a halt, sah."

The Chief Constable was speaking to Brigadier Chamber-Renton, "As far as we can ascertain, Peter, your chap Major O'Brien didn't get off the train at Kings Cross. The Metropolitan lads had the main concourse flooded with their chaps, both in uniform and in civvies. Despite your Major being in military attire he wasn't spotted. He might well, of course, got changed into civilian clothing. The London lads are checking the train's CCTV as we speak to see if he was actually on board the train when it arrived at the terminus, or if he got off before reaching London i.e. Reading, something like that. Oh, and we're trying to get hold of Virgin Train's Ticket Inspector, but there's been a bog standard staff change-over at the terminus and he's wandered off somewhere, which is adding to our difficulties. I'll keep you in the loop though," said the Chief Constable, ringing off.

"A right balls up - typical 'Plod.' They couldn't organise a piss up in a brewery,'" thought the Brigadier.

Knowing that by now, someone would almost certainly be searching for him, and not wanting to be spotted whilst queueing in the station taxi rank where he would have stuck out like a sore thumb, Major O'Brien walked around the corner from the railway station, flagged down a passing taxi and jumped on board. "Morning, Guv. Where to?" asked the driver. "The Chinese Embassy, please," replied O'Brien. "Right you are, Guv," said the cheerful driver, "Come far 'ave yer?"

Twenty minutes late the taxi drew up outside the front entrance of the Embassy of the People's Republic of China, in Portland Square. "That'll be Eighteen quid, please guv," said the taxi driver. Major O'Brien slid him a twenty pound note and said, "Thank you, driver. Keep the change," then jumped out of the taxi.

As the taxi drew away, O'Brien checked his waist belt to ensure that his pistol was still in place. His heart sank to his boots - it wasn't. He realised that somewhere along the journey, either on the train or in the taxi, the weapon had slid out without him noticing. Furious with himself, he strode off, cursing, towards the Embassy entrance. He didn't have a plan about what to do next, so would just try to wing it. If he couldn't use a weapon on Weng then he would use his fists or anything else that he could get his hands on. He was determined to knock seven bells out of Captain Weng, but Major O'Brien wasn't thinking logically.

"Ah, good morning, sir, how may I help you?" asked the pretty Chinese Embassy Receptionist, Fay Moon Cheng. A noticeably perspiring and decidedly edgy Major O'Brien replied, "Young lady, I am Major Peter O'Brien of the British Army, and I would like to speak to your Captain Weng, immediately, please."

The Receptionist smiled and covertly pressed a hidden alarm switch beneath the counter, before replying, "Captain Weng?" She shook her head, "I'm afraid that there is no-one here of that name, sir. Are you sure that you have the right person?"

O'Brien snorted, "Well, I happen to know that he is here, and that he arrived here today! Now, I haven't got time for silly delaying tactics, young lady, so please go and get him for me. Oh, and it might help if you tell him that it is Major Peter O'Brien who wants to speak to him!" "Just one moment, sir," replied Fay Moon as she turned away from the window, picked up the 'phone and rang Agent Fong, the Embassy's Senior Security Officer.

"Agent Fong, it's Fay Moon Cheng. There is a gentleman here at the front desk, asking for Captain Weng. Yes, it was me that pressed the emergency bell. There is something not quite right about him, he seems to be right on the edge. Says that is name is Major Peter O'Brien and he is wearing Army uniform." "Did he say what he wanted Weng for?" asked Agent Fong. "Only that he had to speak to Captain Weng immediately, he didn't say anything else. Believe me, Agent Fong, he is very agitated and looks as if he is about to kick off."

"Well, in that case, I'd better come down and speak to O'Brien myself and see if I can discover what he really wants. Send him over to one of the secure interview rooms, please. I'll warn the security guards off. Offer him a cup of tea or something, it might help to calm him down."

Fay Moon Cheng turned to face the window, "Major O'Brien, a member of staff will come and speak to you about this matter. If you'd care to go and wait for him in Room Three, just over there behind you," she said, pointing, "he will be with you very shortly." "Is it Weng?" asked O'Brien. Fay Moon Cheng shook her head, "No sir, it is Mister Fong. There is no one here by the name of Weng, let me assure you." "Bloody wafflers," mumbled O'Brien as he walked across to Room Three.

CHAPTER ELEVEN

'INTERVIEW WITHOUT COFFEE'

"May I get you something to drink whilst you are waiting, Major? Tea, coffee, water, perhaps?" asked a decidedly nervous Fay Moon Cheng. Major O'Brien shook his head, "No thank you. I just want to speak to Captain Weng." "As I've already told you, someone will be with you in a moment, sir," she said and left him alone in the Interview Room. As O'Brien gazed around the somewhat spartan room, he saw a large mirror fixed to the wall and instinct told him that it was two-way and that he was being watched through it. The only other decoration in the room was a large black and white portrait of an imperious looking Chairman Mao Zedong, staring down at him accusingly and surrounded by a chipped gilt frame.

After ten minutes or so, the door opened and a surprisingly tall Agent Fong came into the room. He sat down opposite Major O'Brien, smiled, then opened a packet of cigarettes, extracted one and lit it. Offering O'Brien one, which he declined, he said, "Major O'Brien. I believe that you wish to speak to someone called Captain Weng?" O'Brien nodded, "That's correct - and please don't try and deny that he's here, because I know for fact that he is, so get him down here, now!"

Dropping his affable attitude, Agent Fong stubbed his half smoked cigarette out on the not too clean Formica table, "Major, may I remind you that to all intents and purposes you are currently on Chinese soil and that you are addressing a senior member of the accredited diplomatic staff. I will not be spoken to as if I am one of your lowly private soldiers! Let us both treat each other with respect, shall we!"

Leaning forward, O'Brien snarled, "Now you listen to me, you Chinese gobshite, I'll talk to you just how I like. Might I remind you that this is London, not Beijing! Now, you'd better go and get Weng before you feel the hairy side of my hand!" An outraged Fong leapt to his feet, knocking his chair over, "Another threat of violence from you, Major, and I shall have the security men throw you out into the gutter where you obviously belong!" As Major O'Brien leapt up on his feet and squared up to Fong, the door suddenly opened and Weng strode into the room.

"Hello, Peter," he said as he walked across the room, picked up the upturned chair and sat on it. He turned to Fong and said, "You may leave us, Fong!" A confused Fong replied, "But Colonel, this man is plainly……" "I told you to leave us!" said Weng. Agent Fong nodded, and said, "Very well, Colonel, but I will be just outside the door if you need me." As Agent Fong left the room he glared evilly at Major O'Brien, then slammed the door shut as he left. "Temper, temper, Fong," murmured O'Brien.

"I warn you; Mister Fong is not a man to offend, Peter," said Weng. "As if I care a flying fart about that, you treacherous, two-faced little swine! And here's me believing that we were friends - and now I hear that you are really a Colonel, not some lowly Transport Captain!" said O'Brien, the bitterness in his voice obvious. Colonel Weng smiled and replied smoothly, "That is correct, but that doesn't change things one iota because I am still your friend, if only you realised it! Don't forget that it's me that has been putting up with your mercurial mood swings for the past several months, when no-one else would. Now, your arrival here is a little unexpected, so why are you here?"

"Why am I here?" said O'Brien, "I'm here because you lied to me about what I was putting on the King's helicopter, that's why! And now, apparently, he is dead!" Weng replied, "But you have done the world a favour!" Suddenly, and without warning, an enraged Major O'Brien jumped up and lunged across the table, grabbing and wrestling a surprised Weng to the floor, then kneeling on his chest, he placed his hands around Weng's throat and started to throttle him.

A superb close contact fighter himself, Colonel Weng executed a swift 'Ba Ji' (*Eight Extremities*) martial arts move, expertly freeing himself from O'Brien's grip and then wrestled him into a hold that prevented any further movement. Weng said, "I advise you to stop this silliness immediately, my friend, or I will break your wrist. You do not seem to realise the enormity of what you're doing!" "Oh, I know full well what I'm doing, you little turd," said O'Brien.

Colonel Weng moved swiftly, increasing the pressure on an expertly administered wristlock, causing O'Brien to gasp out loud with pain, and still unable to move. "You should listen closely to what I have to say next, Peter, my friend!" said Weng, placing his lips next to O'Brien's ear and whispering, "You should be aware that I am a double agent and I am actually working for your MI5! I cannot tell you more as we are being watched from behind the mirror."

"That's pure bullshit!" hissed O'Brien, "Have you forgotten, because I haven't, that you were the main instigator in the murder of King George - and those other innocents that were travelling with him!" Shaking his head, Weng replied, "Yes, that was most unfortunate, but I'm afraid that it was unavoidable collateral damage. Anyway, don't forget that you had a hand in it too, my friend." "Yes, but I didn't know that I was planting explosives. You lied to me. You told me that the metal case was just a piece of electronic jamming equipment - not a bomb!"

Weng laughed, "Well no-one in their right mind's going to believe that, are they!" He leant forward and said quietly, "You see, Peter, for more years than I care to remember, I have trodden a very thin line, having been a most valuable deep cover double agent for the British MI5. Recently, though, I felt that my activities were about to be uncovered by our Security Services, so when I was given the task of assassinating your King, I was unable to refuse without revealing my true loyalties. Now, when I return to China, having got rid of King George, I will have the complete trust of my superiors and have already been promised a promotion to Senior Officer, which will automatically give me access to all sorts of high-grade classified material that will be of great use to your Government. Need I say more ……? I will now stop whispering."

"Can you let go of my wrist, please," said O'Brien. "Only if you promise to calm down and behave yourself!" said Weng. "You have my word!" said O'Brien. Weng released him, then they both stood up and regained their seats. "Now listen carefully, Peter, because we have very little time left," said Weng, glancing at the two-way mirror, "Agent Fong will be wondering what is happening in here. Fortunately, he isn't the sharpest tool in the box, so just play along with what I am about to do and say, please."

A confused Major O'Brien shook his head, "I just don't know what to believe. I feel as if I'm in the middle of some sort of nightmare, one in which I don't know my arse from my elbow! I really trusted you; you know - now look what's happened to me."

Colonel Weng smiled, "Just stick with it for a little while longer, Peter, my friend." Weng reached into his inside jacket pocket and withdrew a small, folded piece of paper, "Here, you must take this with you when you leave here." He slipped the piece of paper to Major O'Brien, who then asked him, "What is it?" "It's the name and telephone number of my contact at your MI5 (*Military Intelligence 5*) department. Read it, memorise it and then eat it!"

"Eat it?" said O'Brien. Weng nodded, "Yes, it's written on rice paper. Now, I am going to have you ejected from the Embassy, so once you are outside and free, I advise you to get in touch with MI5 immediately using the number that I have just given you, and everything will be sorted out for you. If you don't want to eat it, tuck it away inside your sock until you're well away from here."

As an even more puzzled O'Brien surreptitiously folded and tucked the piece of paper inside his stocking top, Weng reached forward and tapped the bell push on the side of the desk. A moment later Agent Fong entered the room, "Yes, sir?" "Agent Fong," said Weng, "I would like you to escort this gentleman off the Embassy grounds, please." A puzzled looking Fong said, "You mean that he is to go free, sir?" Weng nodded, "Yes, you see it appears that Major O'Brien hasn't been very well lately and he now wishes to return to his Army unit to seek medical advice for his, shall we say, mental 'condition.'" "Very well, sir," said Fong.

Turning to Major O'Brien, Fong said, "Major, if you'd care to follow me, please." O'Brien stood up and as he walked out of the room, Weng winked at him and waved goodbye. "Agent Fong is an idiot," thought Weng, "He didn't even think to query how Major O'Brien knew that I was here in the Embassy in the first place. Startling lack of initiative. High time for Fong to be replaced and returned home I think."

Five minutes later Agent Fong, (who was actually Lieutenant Shang Wei of the Chinese Ministry of State Security), returned to the Interview Room and said, "Sir, that's the English Major safely on his way. Incidentally, there was a Metropolitan Police people carrier and several armed policemen waiting for him outside the front of the Embassy. They apprehended and searched him, threw him into their vehicle and then drove off at high speed."

Weng nodded and smiled, "I know, Fong, it was me that sent for them. Excellent. The poor man fell for the standard 'double agent' ploy, hook line and sinker. Ha, ha, the look on his face. You know, Fong, I'd pay a fortune just to see his superior's faces when he starts trying to explain that one to them!" They both sniggered, "Might I tempt you to a drink of refreshing tea, sir?" asked Fong. "Madness not to," said Weng." "Yorkshire Tea, I take it, sir?" "But of course," said Weng.

"Oh, hello sir, it's Sergeant Roy Troth here. We've finally got our hands on the devious bastard. He strolled out of the Chinese Embassy as bold as brass, big gormless grin all over his face. Between you and I, I don't think that he's the full shilling. God alone knows what he's been up to in there. That was a very 'andy tip from the taxi driver who handed the Major's pistol in. Saved us a lot of man hours searching for it. So, we've got his weapon and, more importantly, we've collared the Major. What would you like me to do with him now?"

Sergeant Troth listened closely as he received his instructions, "Right, so hand him and the weapon over to MI5, sir, and they'll handle everything from there. They'll be expecting us. Right you are, sir, I'll crack on with that asap then."

"Ah, my dear Major O'Brien, we meet at last!" said an erudite and very smooth James Adler, a staffer in MI5. "I'm James Adler." They shook hands. "So, I hear that you've had a very interesting few days, culminating with today's visit to the Chinese Embassy. Such affable people the Chinese, don't you think? Now, perhaps you would you like to tell me precisely what's been going on?" Major O'Brien smiled and said, "Before I do, sir, Weng Hang Soon, a name that you might be familiar with, who is currently at the Chinese Embassy, and who is really on our side, slipped me a note with the name and number of his contact here at MI5 written on it. He told me to speak to the man who's name and telephone number is on there and that he'd sort everything out. I didn't get chance to place a call to him myself because 'Plod' grabbed me outside the Chinese Embassy, arrested me, frisked me and brought me straight here."

"May I have a look at the said piece of paper?" asked Adler, holding his hand out. O'Brien extracted the piece of paper from his stocking top and passed it over to him. After glancing at it, James Adler turned to the tough looking man mountain stood immediately behind him and passed the slip of paper over to him, "Harry, go and get these details checked out for me will you, please." Harry nodded, "Right you are, boss. Back in five," and left the room. "Why not let's have a cuppa whilst we're waiting, eh?" said Adler.

When Harry returned, two cups of tea later, he bent over and whispered something in James Adler's ear, "Excuse me boss, the info written on the note. Turns out that it's the telephone number of the 'Wun Meng Chinese Restaurant' in Soho, and the name is that of the owner, a Junfeng Qiaufan. He's not on our books, bass, and as far as we can tell he's never had anything to do with us. Looks like a bum steer to me," he said. Adler nodded, "OK Harry, thanks for that."

Adler looked across at Major O'Brien, smiled at him and waved the piece of paper in the air. "Thanks for this, Major. You'll be pleased to know that it all checks out. Now, what we'd like to do is send you back to your unit so that you can get everything sorted out. Oh, and you'll be delighted to know that your pistol was found in the back of a London taxi and handed in to the Metropolitan Police. And before you ask, no, I'm afraid that you can't have it back. It - and the blank rounds you were carrying on your person will be held here in our Armoury until we can get them couriered back to your unit. In the meantime, I'd like you to go and have a wee chatette with our M.O. (*Medical Officer*) and she'll give you the once over, just to make sure that you're firing on all cylinders. That OK with you?"

Major O'Brien nodded, "Suppose it'll have to be, although I don't really see the need for me to see a Medic. I feel perfectly OK. If you could just put me on the train to Hull, I'll just report back to my unit where I'll face the music and explain everything that's happened, to my boss, the Brigadier. He'll understand."

Adler smiled again and shook his head, "I'm afraid that's not going to happen, old chap. You see, like the Army, we operate under strict guidelines and procedures here. So, in accordance with those guidelines, you'll be seeing our M.O. first and then if she says that you're good to go, we'll send you off, under escort, to Leconfield in an MI5 vehicle." Adler turned to the man stood next to him and said, "Harry, would you kindly take Major O'Brien down to our Medical Centre, please. The Duty Doctor is waiting there to examine him. Major, if you wouldn't mind accompanying Harry, he'll look after you."

Adler stood up then shook hands with O'Brien, "Good luck with everything, old chap," he said, "lovely to have met you - and thanks for this valuable information," he said, waving the little note in the air. Before O'Brien had chance to reply or ask any further questions, Harry grabbed him by the arm and edged him forcefully out of the room. Once the door had closed, Adler smiled, screwed up the note and threw it into the waste bin. He laughed, "The 'Wun Meng Chinese Restaurant' in Soho. Poor Major O'Brien, they certainly saw you coming."

Adler then picked up the 'phone, "Connect me to the Duty Doc will you please, Donna," he said. After a short pause he was connected to the MI5 Medical Centre, "Hi Doc," said Adler, "Major O'Brien's on his way down to see you right now. Harry's bringing him. He's as nutty as a fruitcake and a bit of a fantasist I'm afraid. You should know that he's coming out with the most amazing and laughable piffle. No, no, the Major, not Harry!"

He sniffed, then continued, "I doubt very much that you'll get much sense out of O'Brien. Sounds to me like the poor chap's had a bit of a breakdown, but I'll leave that for you to decide, you're the highly qualified Sawbones after all. Once you've completed his medical examination he's then to be taken under armed escort straight to one of our safe houses out at Farnham where he'll be our guest for a couple of weeks. Considering what he's been involved in, he needs to be properly debriefed. Once that's been done our 'Lords and Masters' will decide what will happen to him. If you can give him a hefty dollop of 'liquid cosh' after his medical examination that would help immensely. We don't want him to be too lively. Harry is sorting the transport details out for his onwards transmission and I'll let his boss, the Commandant of the Defence School of Transportation, know what's going on." He continued, " Now then, Doc, before you ring off, would you like to come and tie on a nosebag with me at the 'The Rag' (*the Army and Navy Club)* later on? My shout!"

He waited for a reply then smiled, "Oh, splendid! It's filet de boeuf én croute tonight, if memory serves," he paused to listen, "Oh yes, of course, I am a silly sausage - you're a Vegetarian. Sorry old girl, totally forgot about that. Well, not to worry, I'm sure that the maître d can get the Master Chef to rustle up a tasty nut cutlet or something like that for you, what! I'm all for healthy options."

CHAPTER TWELVE

'IT'S NOT MY BAG'

"You see, old chap," said King George, "Unfortunately, I didn't realise it at the time, but I was at my absolute happiest when I was the Prince of Wales. To be perfectly honest, deep down in my soul I never really wanted to be King. Apart from it being an obvious 'promotion' and an unavoidable increase in my overall responsibilities, more importantly it meant that I would have lost my dear Mother, the Queen. That was something I truly dreaded and which of course eventually happened. So, now the 'buck stops here' and all that sort of thing. As for my Coronation, don't know if you watched it on TV, well I hated that almost as much as I did the 'Prince of Wales' anointing ceremony. That sort of thing's just not my bag, you see - and that bloody State Coach we used to get to and from Parliament was a nightmare. It rolled around the Mall like a drunken sailor. At one stage the Queen very nearly up chucked! So it's not been the cake walk that everyone thought it was."

"Well, you say all that, er Your Royal Highness, er, Majesty, er sir," said Dan. The King smiled, "Please, Dan, just call me George." "Well, George, I'm afraid that those are the cards you've been dealt with. Face it, you could have been earning a living on the bins, or down a coalmine, or even worse - been a politician!" said Dan. Steph chipped in, "Being the King can't be all that bad, and you're one of the richest men in the world apparently! It said in the Sunday papers that you're a billionaire, that alone must make everything worthwhile. You can do anything you want to, go anywhere you want to, buy anything you want to."

The King nodded and replied, "Yes, Steph, but that's a common misconception don't you see. All the bowing and scraping, the jewels, the palaces, the cars - in real terms, they're not mine - they're yours." "Well, the Crown Jewels might be, but Sandringham, Balmoral and Windsor aren't ours, are they?" said Steph, "You know what George, me and Dan had to pay an arm and a leg just to get into the Royal Mews at Buckingham Palace last year to have what turned out to be a quick look around before we were ushered out. Bloody scandalous! After all's said and done, we, the public, paid for all of that stuff in the first place." "Oh no! You've sent her off on one of her rants now, George," said Dan.

"But the entrance money that you paid is used for the upkeep of the Royal Mews, don't you see," replied the King, "and as for Sandringham, Balmoral and Windsor - well, one has to have a decent roof over one's head, doesn't one. Anyway, I've given the matter a great deal of thought whilst I've been 'convalescing' here and I have decided to wash my hands of the whole blessed 'Royal' business. I'm going to Abdicate. Yes, I'm standing down."

"Well, that's bloody charming, innit, George," said Steph, "You can't just jack everything in just because things have got a bit difficult, surely? And what about your young lad, Prince James, eh! That'll mean he'll cop for the lot." The King smiled, "That won't be a problem for him. he's full of vim and vigour and much more determined than I, is our Jimbo. He'll take to the Kingship like a duck to water. I had to wait for far too long, don't you see. When I was younger I had the best of both worlds and now I'm too set in my ways. It's high time for me to step aside and gently fade from the scene."

"Time to step aside!" exploded Steph, "You've only been at the job for two bloody minutes! Your Mother was our Monarch for nigh on seventy years. If you want my opinion," said Steph, "you want to get a grip of yourself, Georgie boy! I don't think that you've thought this through properly. Don't forget that you've had a bit of a shock and you're not thinking clearly. We, i.e. your people, love and respect you and your Queen. All that we ask in return is that you do your job to the best of your ability, shaking hands and dishing out knighthoods etc. We don't expect you to rule the nation with an iron hand like Henry the Eighth! Just get on with it, like your late Mother did. God bless her."

"Bloody hell fire," said Dan, "There endeth the first lesson!" "Well," said an indignant Steph, "he started it with all that silly Abdication talk!"

"Look, sir, she's right you know. Perhaps you just need a bit more time to think about all of this? It's a big step to take you know," said Dan. The King shook his head, "No, I've made my mind up, Dan. I just need to discuss it with Queen Margaret and see what she thinks." "I doubt she'll be over the moon," said Dan.

Steph sighed, "So, you want to earn a living fishing for lobsters out of Bridlington or something low key like that then, eh. And how long do you think you'll be able to do it without someone recognising you and spoiling everything? The place is full of holidaymakers and some of them will have seen you before. They'll make your life a misery. And anyway, who's going to press your shoelaces, squeeze the toothpaste onto your toothbrush and serve you a full English breakfast every morning! You'll never manage all that sort of stuff by yourself. You're just not used to it."

"I damn well will, Steph," said George, stamping his foot, "as long as I have Margaret at my side. And all that business about toothpaste and having my shoelaces pressed is stuff and nonsense generated by the mischievous media to try and make me look foolish. It's very unfair of them. Anyway, I do not have my shoe laces pressed. I always wear slip-ons or casual loafers!" said a defiant George.

He continued, "Regarding work, I was taught a lot of useful things whilst I was a young lad at Gordonstoun you know, stuff like building brick walls and hanging gates," "That'll come in very handy on a lobster boat," said Steph. Ignoring her, George continued, "And I was in the Andrew (*Royal Navy*) for a couple of years, you know! Even captained my own ship - the HMS Bronington, a Ton-class minesweeper." "A minesweeper, eh. Oooh, you'll be able to do sweeps of Bridlington harbour on the 'Yorkshire Belle,' said Steph.

"Give it a rest with the sarcasm, Steph," said Dan, "it's not funny. Go and put the kettle on, love, whilst I have a chinwag with the King."

"Hang on a mo, I've had an idea. Why don't I make the tea?" said George brightly, jumping to his feet, "I saw dear Papa do it once, so I'm sure that I could cook us a brew. Have you got a strainer?'" Steph sighed, "Sit down, bonny lad, you're as bad as Dan is. Stay right there and I'll sort it out. Biscuits?" George smiled, "Oh, that would be rather yummy."

CHAPTER THIRTEEN

'DOUBLE DEALING'

"Good morning. Hull Daily Mail switchboard. Melanie speaking, how may I help you?" asked the telephone operator, trying not to sound too bored. "Oh, hello Melanie, is that the news desk?" "No sir, it's the Hull Daily Mail switchboard. Would you like to speak to someone on the news desk?" she enquired. "Yes please. Preferably someone who deals with Royal stories." The Operator replied, "I'll put you through to our Chief Reporter, Tom Broadfoot, then. He covers most of the Royal stuff. Er, whom shall I say is calling?" "He won't know me, but you can tell him that it's Dan Clayton." "Hold on a moment please, Mr Clayton."

"Morning, Mr Clayton, Tom Broadfoot here. Sorry to keep you waiting. What can I do for you today then?" "Well, Mr Broadfoot, Tom, before I begin, let me assure you that what I am about to tell you might sound rather hard to believe, but every word of it is true, and let me assure you that I am not a nut job." "OK," said Tom, not believing a word Dan said and reaching across to switch his tape recorder on, "Go on then, fire away."

"Before I do, let me assure you that this story will definitely be a headline grabber and you will more than likely become a Pulitzer Prize winner as a consequence of having your name associated with it. Yes, you'll more than likely become rich and famous overnight," said Dan. "Oh, really," said Tom, whilst thinking, "Why is it always me that attracts loony tunes?" "Before I say another word, though," said Dan, "I want to know what's in it for me?"

"Depends on what story you're going to tell me, Mr Clayton - and, more importantly, if you've got any evidence, photographic or otherwise to support it." said Tom. "Oh, I've got something better than photos, I've got the real thing," said Dan. "OK, let's hear it then," said Tom. "Now, you're never going to believe who my current house guest in Beverley is, Tom, …." "It's not Elvis is it?" said Tom. "Listen, if you're going to be flippant," said Don, "I can just as easily give this story to the Sun!" "Sorry, I didn't mean to sound facetious, I was just trying to lighten things up a bit," said Tom, "please continue."

"Well, said Dan, "My wife Steph and I, or should that be me, were out on the beach doing a bit of metal detecting you see, when Steph saw what looked like a tailor's dummy rolling around in the surf, so I went across to investigate, like you do - and you'll never guess what I found rolling in the surf."

CHAPTER FOURTEEN

'PRESIDENT XI JIANG HO WILL SEE YOU NOW'

"Pardon me, Mister President." The haughty President Xi Jiang Ho, looked up, removed his spectacles and then rubbed the two red marks at the top of his nose with his thumb and forefinger. He had recently decided to have his eyes lasered so that he wouldn't have to wear spectacles but hadn't yet found the time to have it done. "Yes, what is it, Ming Zi?" he asked impatiently.

"Lieutenant General Tang Zhi Peng has arrived in the outer office, Mister President," said Lieutenant Colonel Jin Ming Zi, the President's fearsome and highly protective Military Attaché and Personal Assistant.

"Oh, he has, has he. Well, let him stew in his own juice for half an hour or so, Ming Zi, and then wheel him in here. Before you do, you must ensure that he does not sit down. Tell him that he is to remain standing, unless I say otherwise!" said the President before replacing his spectacles and turning to watch Sky News on the huge screen that was hanging on the wall at the side of his desk. The news was all about King George the Seventh being involved in a helicopter accident. The President tutted loudly.

In the outer office, Lieutenant General Tang's spindly legs were trembling with excitement. He was convinced that today was the day that he would be promoted to full General and, if he were really lucky, the President would pin one of the grateful nation's highest awards, 'The Medal of Army Brilliance' on his ancient chest - indeed, why not both. He was gasping for a cigarette but knew better than to light up as the President disapproved of other people smoking in his presence, although he occasionally smoked himself.

Tang desperately needed to go to the lavatory and also wanted to take the weight off his ancient weary and trembling legs for a few minutes, but, quite insultingly in his opinion, had not been granted permission to do so. He would just have to stand there and wait.

After some thirty minutes had passed, a light flicked on at the side of the Military Attachés desk. Lieutenant Colonel Jin Ming Zi stood up and said, "General Tang, it is now time for your interview with our beloved President. Before we enter the President's inner sanctum, may I have your personal weapon please!" he held his hand out. The General smiled, "Of course," then slid the pistol from the side holster hanging from his highly polished waist belt, unloaded it, removed the magazine and handed it to Jin.

"I will look after it until after the President has finished with you, General," said Jin, "Now, follow me please - and General, do not speak unless the President asks you a question, and you are not to sit down unless the President invites you to do so."

"Mister President, Lieutenant General Tang Zhi Peng!" The President nodded and then waved his Attaché out of the room. Lieutenant General Tang shuffled into the room, saluted and stood rigidly to attention, (as much as he could do with his stoop), in front of the President's desk. "Any moment now," he thought, "I will be invited to take a seat and receive my accolades."

"Ah, General Tang. You must be asking yourself why you are here today? Perhaps it is to receive a long awaited promotion or be awarded a nice shiny medal." "At last, here it comes," thought a thrilled and smiling Tang. The President continued, "Well, you would be quite wrong, because immediately after this meeting, you will be taken out of here and placed under close arrest."

The General's jaw dropped and he wondered momentarily if the President was having a joke at his expense, if so it was a very poor joke. "Did I hear you correctly, Mister President, or are my ears playing tricks?" gasped the General.

The President nodded, "Yes, you heard me correctly. I could have had you arrested earlier this morning but I wanted the joy of breaking the news to you personally." "But what have I done wrong, Mister President?" asked the astounded General. "What have you done wrong? You should be asking what it is that you haven't done wrong! You have failed me, and by doing so you have failed this great nation of ours."

General Tang, who was now feeling quite faint, pleaded, "This comes as a great shock. May I take a seat, Mister President?" "No, you may not!" came the acid reply, "What you can do for me is repeat the motto of our greatly cherished Secret Service!" "Our motto, Mister President?" replied a puzzled Tang. "Yes," replied the President, "your motto!" "Very well, Mister President," said the General,

"The Secret Service motto is"

'Serve the People' firmly and purely, reassure the party, be willing to contribute, be able to fight hard and win.

"Word perfect!" said the President, icily, "And now, perhaps you can explain 'why' you have failed me?" "Failed you? In what way have I failed you, Mister President?" asked the General. "Without consulting me or obtaining my express permission, you arranged for the assassination of the despised King George the Seventh!" "But Mister President!" pleaded Tang.

"Do not dare to interrupt me!" roared Xi Jiang Ho. "Not only did you fail to seek my permission for the operation, but your operative failed to remove him from the face of the earth. Are you aware that the British King is still alive!?"

Tang gasped, "It cannot be true, Mister President. I have it on good authority that he was blown to pieces!" said a plainly shocked Tang. The President shook his head, "No actually, he wasn't! He survived the explosion, and the crash that followed it. I also have it on good authority that he is alive and well and skulking with his oppressed people somewhere up in a place called East Yorkshire! You have failed me personally and by your unauthorised actions you have placed the Chinese nation in great jeopardy. The British will most definitely do something about this! Be under no allusion that there will be serious repercussions. They have already despatch two of their nuclear submarines towards the South China Sea. Any fool knows that you do not tinker with the British Royal Family!" roared the President, slamming his open hand onto his desk, startling the General, "and not only that, somehow the despicable British MI5 has managed to link the assassination attempt directly to us, I believe via the unauthorised actions of one of your obviously grossly inefficient operatives, Weng Hang Soon!"

The General sank to his ancient, trembling knees, "But Mister President, the operation went ahead exactly as planned." "You are a simpering old man! How could it have done if that bumbling fool Windsor still draws breath! Look - they are even talking about the attempt on Sky News! The whole world is outraged and there is even talk of me being branded a war criminal. Me!"

The President paused to light a cigarette, "Because of you and your department's abject incompetence, to make amends, I am going to have to invite the King and his paramour here on a 'State Visit' at which great amounts of humble pie will be eaten and I will be required to apologise and explain that because of your senile decrepitude you had a mental aberration and went totally off piste! Now get back up onto your feet! It is time for your services to be dispensed with."

The General struggled back up onto his feet, gasping for breath. "Mister President, may I respectfully remind you that I have served you, your predecessors and, more importantly, China to the very best of my ability, for more years than I care to remember. One mistake, that is all I have made. Can I not at least be allowed to return to my village and fade away quietly for what little remains of my life?"

The President shook his head, "No, you may not. I, we, need a scapegoat - and you, General Tang - or should I say soon to be ex-General Tang, will be it. There is no room for manoeuvre in this matter. Someone is going down, and that someone isn't going to be me. I have already decided that your services are no longer required and that you will be 'dispensed with' immediately after this interview!"

"Very well, Mister President." said Tang, "Then if that is to be my fate then might I be permitted to make one last request?" he asked. The President nodded, "You may." "My operative, Weng Hang Soon, who organised the King's assassination attempt, was only doing his duty and obeying my express orders. The failure of this operation is down to me, not him. Weng is a brave, loyal and faithful officer who does not deserve to be punished," he added defiantly, "and if anything he should be promoted and given a medal!"

The President leaned back in his chair, steepled his fingers and smiled, "Too late, I'm afraid, General. The unfortunate Weng was arrested at roughly six o'clock this morning, whilst you were 'sleeping' with your apparently very pretty assistant, who has also been arrested, incidentally!" The President looked at his wristwatch, "Now, have you anything else to say before I have you removed from my presence. You offend me."

The General doing his best to look dignified, stood to attention and said quietly, "I would just like to say for the record, Mister President, that you are an unprincipled, cowardly and ungrateful swine who is not fit to lead our beloved nation, unlike your beloved father!" As he was speaking, General Tang gently shook his right arm and a wickedly sharp commando knife slid down into his hand, unseen by the President.

"How dare you address your President in such a disrespectful and insulting manner!" roared Xi Jiang Ho, jumping up onto his feet, whilst at the same time pulling open his desk drawer and reaching inside it for a loaded pistol that was always kept in there, loaded, for immediate use in the event of emergencies, "For your gross impertinence, I will despatch you myself!"

As the President looked away from the General momentarily in order to cock his pistol, General Tang suddenly turned sideways, raised his arm and expertly threw the knife at the President. The knife hurtled towards the President, suddenly stopping in mid-air and bouncing harmlessly to the floor. General Tang gasped in amazement. The President smiled, "You may know many things, General, but you obviously don't know that I am protected at all times in here by a room sized sheet of bullet proof glass which sits at the edge of my desk. One can never be too careful these days, can one!"

General Tang, stood there, drooling and his mouth hanging slack. The President said, "I should close my mouth if I were you, General, otherwise it will be filled with flies! Now, in view of your treachery and the fact that you alone have brought Great Britain and China to the very edge of conflict, you must be punished. Up until now, as far as I am aware, you have been a faithful and loyal servant to the State, so I have decided that you will not be executed. You are demoted with immediate effect and will be taken from here to the far North West of the country, to a Xinjiang Internment/Re-Education Camp to be precise. A fine example of a Vocational Education and Training Centre, although you will be allocated a menial task there. You will remain at the Centre for what is left of your miserable life. Incidentally, I have arranged for you to share a cell with Weng Hang Soon, seeing as how you are both such good friends. That will be fun."

The smiling President continued, "By the way, whilst you are there, you will come under the authority of the powerful Provincial Standing Committee of which my son-in-law, Duan Lee Young, is Chairman. I'm sure that he will be keeping a watchful eye on you both." The President then reached forward and pressed a bellpush that was on the corner of his desk. His Military Attaché entered the room, "Mr President?" "Ah, Ming Zi, take this miserable object away and hand him over to the prison guards will you." His MA nodded and grabbed hold of ex-General Tang's arm, "Come with me, Tang!" he ordered.

As they left the room, the President said, "Oh, and Ming Zi, when you have disposed of that object, you can come back in here and explain to me how

Tang managed to bring a weapon into the room!" "But Mister President, I have Tang's pistol safely locked away in my safe," replied Ming Zi. The President pointed to the wicked looking knife on the floor in front of his desk. "Did you search him?" The shamefaced Military Attaché shook his head. He would be lucky to wriggle out of this one, he thought. Tang just sniggered.

CHAPTER FIFTEEN

' IS THIS BUCKINGHAM PALACE? '

"Your Majesty!" "Your Majesty!" "Waken up please, sire!" King George slowly opened his eyes, stretched and yawned. Standing directly in front of him and gently shaking the King's shoulder was his ever loyal Equerry, Major Adrian Longman QGM. "Adrian, is that you making all that infernal racket?" asked the King. "Yes, Your Majesty, 'tis I," replied a smiling Major Longman, "Well, kindly desist!" said the King. "Forgive me, sire, but it is entirely necessary," replied Longman.

The King gazed slowly around the room and after a few moments asked the Major, "Er, might seem a bit of a daft question, but is this Buckingham Palace or Beverley, Ade?"

The Equerry, looking confused, nodded and replied, "Why, it's Buckingham Palace, of course, sire," whilst thinking, "Oh no, he's gone off on one again. It's going to be one of those days, I can feel it in my water."

"Er, is everything alright? You feeling OK, sire?" he asked politely. The King nodded and smiled, "Yes, I'm perfectly fine thanks. Tell you what though, Ade, I feel as if I've just been trapped in someone else's dream, albeit an amazingly colourful and realistic one." The Equerry smiled knowingly, "Ah, so Your Majesty has been taking a little 'zizz' then?" The King grinned, nodded and then asked him, "Yes, it appears that I have. Incidentally, Ade, does my nose look all right to you." "Alright? Your nose?" asked the puzzled Equerry. "It's not bent out of shape or anything, is it?" said the King.

The Major looked even more puzzled, "Bent out of shape? Is this a trick question, sire?" "No, of course it isn't!" replied the King, "Does my nose look OK to you? Yes or No!" he asked again.

Major Longman took a long and searching look at the King's nose. "It looks OK to me, sire, in point of fact it's a fine Hanoverian protuberance, if I might be so bold, Your Majesty?" "So my conk isn't damaged in any way. Not even a scratch??" asked the King. "No. It looks perfectly fine to me, sire. There might be the odd old polo injury, but nothing that jumps out at one."

The Equerry glanced down at his wristwatch, "Er, Your Majesty, I hate to put the arm on you, but I have been asked to give you a respectful reminder that you are now a few minutes late boarding the helicopter. If we delay leaving here for very much longer, we might just lose the RAF's 'Purple Passage' clearance,'" said the Major.

"The helicopter? What bloody helicopter?" asked the puzzled King. "The Sikorski that's flying you up to East Yorkshire for yours and Her Majesty's visit to the Defence School of Transportation 'DST' at Leconfield. It's parked up at the back of the palace, waiting for you."

Suddenly, the King went as white as a sheet, and he shot up onto his feet, "Thunderation, 'DST' Leconfield you say!" The Equerry nodded, "Yes, it's 'Oop' in East Yorkshire, sire." The King paused for a moment, then said, "Yes, I know where it is, thank you, Ade." He paused for a moment then asked, "So, where is the Queen at this precise moment in time?" "Her Majesty is sat on board the helicopter, waiting for you to join her there, sire." "Oh, is she," said the King.

He continued, "Right, well, I'm calling for an immediate change of itinerary, Ade. You'd better nip off and tell Margot to remove herself from the chopper and to pop straight up here so that I can explain what's going on to her, and why."

"Are we not travelling 'Oop North' then, sire?" asked the puzzled Equerry. The King shook his head, "No, I mean yes, well, not by helicopter anyway. I've decided that we'll all travel up to Yorkshire on board the Royal Train."

The Equerry was aghast, "The Royal Train, Your Majesty! But, but it's been stored away in the siding at Wolverton Works for weeks. It won't be prepared!" "Well, do a bit of name-dropping and pull a few strings with the Train Manager. Order him to get the bloody thing cranked up; I mean that's what he gets the big bucks for isn't it? Er, tell him that there's OBE's in it for him and his boss if he sparks! Now, go and fetch the Queen, please, - oh, and you'd better order the chopper to return to base, we won't be needing it for the foreseeable future. They can pencil today's gig in as being a training flight, that'll keep the bean-counters quiet. Go on then, Ade - shoo! The clock's ticking! "

"Right away, Your Majesty," said Major Longman, bowing then scuttling from the room as fast as his feet would carry him.

"On the bus, off the bloody bus. Nothing's ever straightforward with Georgie boy," thought Major Longman. As he ran down the palace stairs, he wondered where the Train Manager would find a driver for the Royal Train at such short notice. It was always a problem getting locomotive drivers these days because they were usually on strike. Perhaps the Army's Royal Logistic Corps might be able to help.

He sighed, knowing that he'd have problems persuading the Queen to exit the helicopter. She was already chilled out, having donned her favourite slippers and was sat back, feet up, happily reading that day's copy of the 'Horse Racing News' and having a quick vape before the King arrived.

After his Equerry had departed at speed, the King flopped back in his chair. "Bloody hell," he thought, "the dream that I just had was so detailed and frighteningly realistic. The only thing that I can think of is that I must have eaten the wrong sort of mushrooms at brekkers. Well, be that as it may, I'm definitely not going to tempt fate. Such warnings are not to be ignored. I think that we'd all be much better and safer travelling by Royal Train for the next few weeks. Good job that I ordered those tight buggers at the Treasury to retain it. They've had the ship, they're not getting the bloody choo-choo as well!"

He sighed, "I must say, though, on reflection, dream or not, I did rather like Dan and Steph. They really went out of their way to look after me," he paused and then licked his lips, "I wonder if my Master Chef knows anything about preparing scraps…."

CHAPTER SIXTEEN

' MIND THE GAP! '

President Xi Jian Ho waved his hand towards a seat and said to General Wen Qian Hong, "General, take a seat and make yourself comfortable." Once the General had sat down, he crossed his legs and made himself comfortable, then waited for the pearls of wisdom that he was sure would pour forth from his President's mouth.

"Firstly, General," said the President, "Allow me to congratulate you on your recent appointment as Head of State Security, the People's Republic of China." "It is a great honour, Mister President," replied the General." "I do hope that you will be more successful than some of your predecessors in State Security," said the President, "several of whom are now gainfully employed in the paddy fields - or are under them!" The General visibly paled and had to fight not to break wind.

The President continued, "So, General, I would like you to brief me about the current state of play regarding 'OPERATION WINDSOR.' Please keep it reasonably short as I have another meeting to attend within the hour." The General stood up and handed a classified folder to the President for him to browse through whilst he, the General, was giving the briefing.

Some thirty minutes later as the briefing drew to a close, the General said, "In essence, Mister President, we have a Royal Train Driver who has been under deep cover for many years and he has been briefed what is required of him when the King boards the train for Yorkshire later today." "He is aware that it is a suicide mission?" asked the President. The General nodded, "Yes, sir."

"And the man's name?" asked the President. "It is Steven Gap, Mister President." "How very appropriate," said the President, "Steven Gap." "Forgive me, sir, but I do not understand the significance of that?" said the General. "Come on, General, you've travelled on London's inferior trains! 'Mind the Gap!'" said the President.

THE END

Terry Cavender

Born in Keighley, West Yorkshire, Terry and his wife Maggie have crossed the great divide and now live in the historic market town of Beverley, East Yorkshire. Since the completion of his most recent time-travel adventure novel, 'Seeking the Ark of the Covenant' Terry has been writing 'God Save the King.'

Terry's other books, of which these are some, are currently available from Amazon/Kindle Books.

  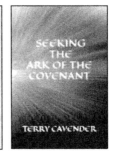

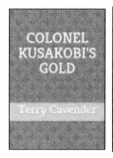

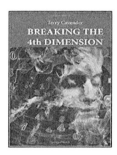

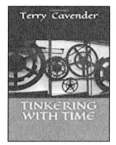

Printed in Great Britain
by Amazon